REDOLENT WIND

Also by Dennis Bove

Oblivion's Whisper: The Winter Portraits
Conducting Fireflies
Endswell
Onondaga Hollow
Random Kings
Reluctant Aerialist
Resplendence Keeper

Purple Earl Meets a Girl

Thanks you to my wife Martha, and my son Seth,
Cordell Reaves, and Kathy Albertson for all of the
fine editing and useful suggestions they have
provided regarding my work ... and to my daughter
Sara for always asking such great questions.

REDOLENT WIND

a novel by

Dennis Bove

A redolent wind pushed me,
fueled by the combined voices of all my ancestors,
the false bravado of some local morning newscaster,
and that jerk down at the local gas station
who gave me an earful
of his loathful bemoaning this morning...
What will become of me, much less the day,
is as ever - unknown.

Peter Atwell Phillips

Death is nothing at all. It does not count.
I have only slipped away into the next room.
Nothing has happened.
Everything remains exactly as it was.
I am I, you are you, and
the old life that we lived fondly together
is untouched, unchanged.

Henry Scott-Holland (1910)

The Troy Book Makers
www.thetroybookmakers.com

ISBN: 978-1-61468-375-9

For Ralph & Rita

He forever watching the water and her
safely shadowed under a wide-brimmed hat

INTRODUCTION

First, let me tell you that I am dead. As dead as a door nail. And, while I agree with Mr. Dickens that a coffin nail may be the most mortal piece of metal on Earth, I am still quite dead. That doesn't mean I can't be the narrator of dear Peter's story. I can, seeing that I now *transcend the indefinite continued progress of other people's existence*, and am actually moving beyond my own time of being. Death is a tricky thing, and not easily explainable to the living - so I'm not even going to try.

Most folks, I suspect, given the opportunity to ask questions, would want to know if I'm in heaven. Is there a sky city surrounded by fluffy clouds and brilliant rainbows or a comfy curtained bed inhabited by seven willing virgins? Recent experience indicates that Elysium is right there in corporeal form, standing with a fragrant summer breeze at your back, under the forgiving gaze of your loved ones. So... embrace and remember that.

Let me also assure you that while I was often pushed about harshly by life during my brief tenure, I always gave back as good as I got. Gratefully, despite the inexplicable turmoil which we all seem to share, I was able to find great love. Sure, much of that hazy serendipity was stolen from me, but even in its staggering loss, I never stopped looking for its replacement. Yes. I am a dead romantic.

My name is Gabriel Mullaney, and as Peter Atwell Phillips' glad raconteur, I will admit to a certain bias regarding the wee lad, as all my recollections of him are totally subjective - burnished by our time spent together and percolated as well through the various screens and filters of our own singular and conjoined histories.

In the telling, be warned that there may be many slight departures and ramblings off-script, especially concerning art and its artists' philosophies and subsequent trends - as this is how my mind often works (well... worked). Where others might watch a field of wheat softly swaying in a breeze and think of a melody, I see their continual shifts of textures as brush strokes in varied hues and tints. In a single strawberry, I can not only taste the sweetness, but smell and touch its bumpy REDNESS. In rare cases, although much more often now, I believe that I can (could) hear colours. Their voices are but tiny whispers - more like gentle afterthoughts - but clear if you take the time to stop and listen.

See. I've already done it and gone off topic... and the story hasn't even begun yet.

Sadly, it was the premature death of my dear Michael that allowed adequate space in my fractured heart for young Peter to move in, as he slowly became my third son. That bittersweet and grateful adaptation will undoubtedly add a brighter hue - even if unintended - to the darker passages of this saga.

The premature deaths of both my dear wife Siobhán (Shi-**vawn**) and my beloved sister-in-law Julia will certainly colour my interpretations of the women - save one - that he's chosen to love. My pleasant years as an Art apprentice will no doubt inform my views of his college terms. The world of war where I wore olive-drab clothing for fear of standing out in the Ardennes Forest will unquestionably shade my view of any anti-war dialogue or his ardent attendance at campus protest rallies. And, those chilled years of self-imposed solitude in the mountains where I worked alone as a painter until Peter and sweet Lorraine entered my tedious life, will also add a golden hue to the patina of my tale.

Peter, you will find, is a good lad. A flawed lad. A misguided and often beguiling lad... and I love him - even from the grave.

PART ONE

The world, as we all know, is a far bigger place than our dear Peter's adolescent home so casually cast in the shadow of Speculator Mountain. The Adirondack land surrounding his birth place was first home to the mighty Iroquois, before the arrogant French trappers and Dutch settlers came and once there refused to leave. That sanguine and secluded spot allowed many acres of uninterrupted walking and included a splendid view of Pleasant Lake - which was a perfect setting for hours of gentle contemplation - OK, daydreaming. That memorable vista was the basis for his first landscape painting, the success of which drew him quickly into the conjoined spheres of both art and philosophy.

You should have seen the look on the poor boy's face when Peter first visited my studio in New York City. I had to literally pop both of his eye balls back into his head. Where he was born, a big city was the size of Lake Placid with a mere twenty-five hundred people calmly wandering around in it (not including tourists). New York City, on the other hand, currently contains a nicely compacted 8.5 million folks - all of whom are fervently vibrating at very different frequencies.

Young Peter was able to attend the prestigious Wainwright Academy for the Arts in downtown Redden, New York, for four full years, mostly through a series of scholarships, and I'm proud to say they were all provided by me. He never knew about my glad donations to the cause. He was only privy to the nonpartisan grants that were submitted on his behalf. This was my idea. At first you'd think me shy and reserved - not wishing to be acknowledged for my kind and generous actions (and you'd be wrong) - but then you'd recognize it was in Peter's best interest for him to think that he'd won enough scholarship money to complete his education - all on his own. My plan was not to deceive him, but to prop up his confidence. "*A man can do just about anything,*" my father Owen used to say, "*if he only has enough confidence to overshadow its impossibility.*"

This tact was in complete opposition to his own father's selfish plans. Atwell Phillips had never once thought to build up his son's self-assuredness. He only sought to exploit the boy's cheap labor and enduring loyalty. The idea of creating a viable foundation under his son's burgeoning psyche through emboldened confidence was as foreign to him as giving coins to charity. Atwell was a hundred and ninety pounds of pure selfishness with absolutely no room for any measure of altruism in him. For the same reasons that nature allowed the origin and evolution of mosquitoes, cockroaches, and venomous snakes, was the person of Atwell Phillips inserted into this world. Some philosophers might argue the need for such a rotten individual as a point of balance, suggesting that *a person can't fully grasp the idea of true goodness without having first experienced its arch reciprocal.* For me, and all my loved ones, I'd prefer to allow our imaginations to have conjured up such a vile beast, and let the duration of such an exposure be far more limited. Poor Peter spent seventeen years wandering around in Atwell's careless abyss.

If memory serves, there was, during his elementary school years, a brief idyllic romance - if only in Peter's own mind. While he liked her right away, she never really saw him as more than just another classmate. The hook for him was simple. Peter'd never seen such a beautiful girl as Gina, for her skin was the colour of a starless night. Before her fortuitous arrival, most folks in his limited world of experience looked just like he did. Gina was a glorious variation and he couldn't take his eyes off of her.

High School for Peter was sort of reminiscent of the film *Footloose*, only without the banned music and forbidden dancing. Sure, Newton's Corners is a small town kind-of-place, but most folks in the Adirondacks love singing and dancing. I can almost hear the fiddles and banjos playing *Blackberry Blossom* at Peter's Junior Prom right now. Like Kevin Bacon's character in the movie, Peter not only got the girl, but he also developed a rather rebellious nature regarding authority. This was both a good and a bad thing. While it helped him to stand up and become his own man, it only heightened his grief at home - for Atwell liked it best when children just did as they were told. The abuse there would only end when Peter was big enough to deflect a slap, and walk out.

Like most folks, I was sure that "happy music" banjos came from the north country. At least that's where I first became aware of them. Their true origin turns out to be from Gina's Angola ancestors. They'd been playing such instruments as the Bami Jo in celebration for hundreds of years, long before those thoughtless men of history colluded to highjack them here to the west bound in chains. Like everything else in this grand country, American folk and bluegrass music came about through the necessity of blended cultures.

Throughout his late teenage years, it seemed to me, that Peter had engaged in a series of monogamous relationships, none of which lasted longer than three months. Looking back at it now, he may have unconsciously been going through an acute calendar phase by selecting these particular women in the order that he did - or (which is my belief) the universe was just messin' with him. His first attraction was to a saucy blonde named Spring Collins who sat in front of him during first period Social Studies. It was his first introduction to both archeology and hallway kissing. Gentle Spring and all her lovely curves was followed in quick succession by the rough and tumble tomboy Summer Brighten. During their shared vacation, Summer taught our impressionable boy a few things about dirty-dancing and creek water skinny-dipping. When Peter's Junior year began in September, he chanced to meet the demure Miss Autumn Draper as they were entering the library together. With very little prompting, Autumn happily showed him what the darkened reference aisles were really meant for - not exactly what librarian Melvil Dewey had in mind for his numbered stacks back in 1876. By graduation, Peter had spent the last few months getting to know Hollie Noelle Winter, who, with her long rolled braids and white lace blouses, sat within arms' reach of him in French class. Along with learning that playfully Romantic tongue of *oui oui* and *magnifique*, they happily explored a new kind of *deep* kissing.

Practice. Practice. Practice, I always say.

While I was at least personally aware of Peter's youthful tomfoolery during his high school years, as I often acted as his default parent whenever Atwell found himself in fatherly disarray, I did not yet possess my current omnipresent powers during his college years. All that I know about that time in his life is what he was willing to share with me. Obviously much of the juicy-bits were left out for my sake, but I can make some educated guesses as to what happened and when.

Having been a rather gangly boy of all elbows and knees, the new and improved adult Peter now has a rather pleasing physique. That is, if I can trust my keen observations of the way that young women admiringly gaze at him. And why shouldn't they, given his broad shoulders, strong chin, and full head of curly auburn hair? He is truly an approachable Adonis. Obviously, my plan to inject some self-assuredness into the lad's marrow has succeeded. Sanguine Peter walks that walk a man of shear confidence walks - while not even remotely being aware that he's doing so. Never a showman's practiced manner or some phony's skillful sham, but one of genuine poise and aplomb that every other man, without even a hint of it, completely covets.

Entering a facility of higher learning can be a good thing. For inspired students, those who've always looked beyond their tiny inner-sanctums, it can be an exhilarating expansion of thought and a path to many unforeseen adventures. For those more sheltered souls, often immersed in the cloak of strict religious dogma, it can bring about true enlightenment - taking that child into the light of boundless inquisitiveness and spirals of free-thinking.

As an incoming freshman, Peter was required to take certain classes that would *round out* his major.

These were courses, of course that were mostly meant to help fund the college and actually offered very little to the student's overall general knowledge. His first period required class was unfortunately proctored by one of the college's least competent instructors. Every university has them - mostly hired through rampant nepotism, where the staff member was totally incapable of obtaining gainful employment on their own merit. This particular professor, Trisha Grassley, taught art history in a manner that was so dry and tiresome that she would've been better suited proctoring a class on willful homicide. Through her lackluster demeanor and deadpan delivery, this dilettante hack managed to succinctly suck the life out of all those heady dead artists we'd grown to love and admire. How in hell could you make Pablo Picasso, René Magritte, and Frida Kahlo seem boring? Somehow she did, by perfectly burying these influential folks and many others under tons of verbal rubble. It was as though she hated their worldly renown in the face of her own stark anonymity. Her equal dislike for Peter was also palpable, for she knew by his daily expressions, that he clearly recognized her foul mendacity. His stalwart gaze could strip her bare with one glance, and she hated him for it.

I overheard Professor Grassley make this rather puzzling statement to an impressionable freshman painting class before nearly passing out myself from boredom: "*you have to be sure to brush the nipple off the tit... .*" I'm not certain what that meant, maybe just an ex-nun's puritanical need to disguise sexual reality - or at its worst - and ode to those wretched Popes who, during The Great Castration, ordered the hacking off or fig-leaf covering of all those splendidly sculpted Greek and Roman penises near the Raphael Rooms at the vatican. Prudish Ms. Grassley went on to say, *"in the middle ages it was understood that only the aberrantly damned were to be found naked, while the enlightened ones, who were perfect and saved - in their rich piousness - always remained fully clothed."* OK... if the *devout* were always so fully clothed like she said, how the hell did they ever reproduce?

Grassley tapped the desk with a short stubby stick, all while staring at her male student's would-be confiscated hardware. Then, with her eyes still diverted, she loudly proclaimed that those Pope's involved were heroes of the faith, doing what needed to be done to protect the people from themselves.

For the record, these unenlightened purveyors of God and forced repressionists were: Pope Paul IV (1555-1559) who's bright idea started all the artistic desecration, Pope Innocent X (1644-1655) - who obviously wasn't that *innocent* - preferring more enduring metal fig leaves over Paul's paltry plaster covers, Pope Clement XIII (1740-1758) - who, in preparation for the future, had fig-leaves mass produced for all the statues within the realm that still brazenly sported free-floating genitalia, and lastly dear Pope Pius IX - who took all the madness one giant leap farther, ordering any sculpture defiantly showing any *man-parts* to be destroyed. Despite what Grassley proclaimed, and given that the human body is considered sacred to most Christians - as having been created in the very image of God, plus the bible quote: *... and may your spirit and soul and body* **be preserved complete** (1 Thessalonians 5:23), there's little chance that some higher power spoke to these deluded fools, calling for such a rampant phallic scouring. It was either a dreaded fear of viewing other men's penises, or simply just another misguided notion - full of false piety - that was forced upon an unsuspecting populous in the name of religion. Do you think a farmer who works hard all day cares one fig if some Greek statue stood around naked? Between all the dangling horses and bulls, any farmer could count the minutes of his day, like inverted sundials, by the number of shadowed penises strolling by.

I'm certain that Jesus never coloured his truths as such, but we'll never really know. Even the *divinely* written words of the Apostles (especially when viewed as them having been embedded news reporters in a Roman vs Christian war zone) were most certainly transmogrified by their own unique and ragged memories causing varied interpretations of the facts. My brother Vincent and I often shared many human happenings in our time together, and when asked about them later, we'd often come up with totally different takes on the very same event. Before they became saints, the twelve were all mere humans like us, and even if, as suggested by some rabid televangelists, were always guided by the very hand of God, still were, by birth, imperfect conduits of truth. How else could the tenor of Jesus's once all inclusive ideas get so skewed that the pontificated dogma arrived at by Pope Innocent X and his ignominious ilk could somehow determine that art could be *obscene* and should be so violently cleansed?

Me... I've always been a science guy. I love all that detailed stuff about paint pigments and how *they change the colour of reflected or transmitted light as the result of wavelength-selective absorption*, while other folks like life in much simpler doses. More mental comfort. Not so much fact. For example, for reasons all their own, some bible-folks suggest that the earth is only six thousand years old, leaving those creationists the opportunity to spout incorrectly that dinosaurs and men shared time on this planet - all while current indisputable geochronological methods indicate that our planet is actually 4.54 billon years old.

A befuddled woman that I met along the rim of the Grand Canyon seemed to know all of the site specific geology, but despite the facts, she was still visibly trapped in the enigma of her faith - having to retain and apply all of those inaccurate biblical time references she'd innocently absorbed as a student.

As an innocent child, I savored the splendid idea of men being able to hang-out with dinosaurs, but as a worldly adult, I now know it just ain't true. To be fair, when their hotel-friendly book was originally written, its hapless scribes didn't have access to all the fine science that we now enjoy. So telling that tall tale about creating the world in just six days was simply one way of explaining things to a highly uneducated populous. Remember how some folks thought that thunder was the result of arguing gods? Well, same thing. Trisha Grassley, like many other unenlightened folks before her, had no business informing young minds with such dreadful drivel - when the real truth was always well within her grasp. We'd have all been better served if she'd had chosen to remain in her dark cloister where the only person she could damage was herself.

Thankfully, a vivacious young blonde named Salome Jørgensen, who was sharing his tedious burden, took Peter's mind off Professor Grassley's dire discourse for a while. Salome, having to read all those tedious historical passages about Greek culture, saw Peter as rather statuesque - a three dimensional illustration if you will. While on his part, historical or not, Peter simply admired her utter voluptuousness. Soon they were spending plenty of time outside the classroom as well.

The lass's perky exuberance and flamboyant nature fit in well with her main course of study - performance art. The only problem with her being an actress was that Peter couldn't always tell when Salome was rehearsing or simply being herself. Throughout their first few weeks together, many major verbal confrontations erupted, each one full of rich drama and vociferous fire - where he wasn't quite sure if it was *she* who was speaking or Eugene O'Neill. Salome's most memorable performances came during their brief tenure of love making - for those nonverbal sparing matches actually contained genuine moments of both passion and intimacy.

The relationship collapsed though, after she delivered a poorly paraphrased soliloquy which she'd freely borrowed from Arthur Miller:

Love, it is God's holy will, and therefore our divine commitment; we are only what we always were, but naked now... Aye, naked!

While Peter thoroughly enjoyed her nudity, he, like myself, always saw the insertion of the godhead into any relationship as a major red warning flag. How could a mere man, with at least a proportional sized penis, hope to compete with an invisible supreme being of massive size and power? So, he left Salome's bed as quickly as he could. She was still performing various elements of *The Crucible* as he left her apartment. A soliloquy, to my understanding, is a literary device usually intended to divulge a character's secret inner workings. In Ms. Jørgensen's case, it often proved instead to be just another brick in her beautiful façade.

As Peter's luck would have it, those odd melodramas mutated into a single glorious adventure - also involving one of the Academy's professors. Unlike that disgruntled hag Grassley, this highly enlightened woman was capable of actually inspiring greatness in her students. The demure Miss Aoife Coghlan (EE-fa KAWG-lun) had been a Catholic nun up until the time that she felt a stronger urge to create rather than blindly serve. Peter liked to imagine that she left the clergy for love of him, but that was simply poor conjecture on his part. Truth be told, and he'd admit it to himself now, his skills at making *whoopee* were poor to middlin' at that time (just ask poor Salome). Hardly worth leaving a well reverenced deity for. Even though he had good instincts and an overwhelming desire to please, like any other skilled activity, there were many fascinating nuances that he'd yet to learn. Thankfully, for the budding sexual novice, Aoife was not only a fine art professor but a patient hands-on instructor in amour as well.

Their relationship grew slowly and didn't come to full fruition until the fall semester of his junior year. Something had happened in Aoife's personal life that'd sent her on a slow downward spiral. Dutiful Peter was there by her side during the darkest days fervently trying to hold her up. A warm and caring embrace can sometimes do that. One thing led to another, and well, like me, you'll have to guess what happened when they found themselves alone in the dark with *Slow Hand* by the Pointer Sisters playing over and over on the turntable. As I mentioned earlier, Peter wasn't always very explicit when he spoke to me at graveside - especially about his dear Aoife.

And no... Peter didn't suddenly get all "A's" in his studio work. Professor Coghlan was above that kind of petty favoritism. But, on occasion, he could guarantee himself a better grade if he chose to use a dab of burnt orange in his composition. Aoife loved burnt orange.

But, this story doesn't begin in The Big Apple, Wainwright Academy, or Peter's tiny Newton's Corners cabin. The bigger world that I previously mentioned also includes the provinces of my beloved niece - Saoirse (Seer-sha) Mullaney.

My tiny world grew by twice its measure when sweet Saoirse was born. She was a beautiful and golden child, full of airy graces and exalted harmony. Just being in her presence gave your troubled life new brightness and buoyancy. It wasn't her fault that my foul brother Vincent aided in giving her life. A child can't choose her parents after all. They can only rebel or resemble their random begetters once they've grown old enough to know them and can make that choice for themselves.

Thankfully, providence had issued a perfect balance in assigning dear Julia to be Saoirse's mother. A published poet in the grandest traditions of her Dorchester home, Julia showered her beloved daughter with the unconditional love she herself had rarely experienced back in England. As I said, no child has ever been able to choose their own birth parents. It's always been a simple roll of the celestial dice.

Snake eyes for poor Julia.

A hard seven for my beloved Saoirse.

Box cars for me.

Knowing what she would later learn about her mother and father (if you could call them that), Julia would never have chosen Lulu and Basil Roth for such important roles in her life. Like Peter's father Atwell, they were absolutely unprepared for the staggering challenges of proper child-rearing. An all consuming hatred for one another left room for only indifference for their innocent and enigmatic daughter.

How did such a vile couple ever manage to conceive a child in the first place, when having sex together was considered an assault on the other's person? Only the fates could explain it - and they're not tellin'. I'm guessing that it was a cruel celestial joke, played sarcastically by a collective of interstellar fools.

Although, against all our forewarnings and the full awareness of what mischief mismatched couples can do to each other, Julia not only chose my vapid brother Vincent to be her awfully-wedded husband, but to also be the father of her child.

Is that the universe laughing - again?

Was marrying Vincent a rebellious act against her own destructive father, for Julia knew full well that Basil sorely hated Vincent? The musician was all false bravado and had such a vile and simpering temperament - so reminiscent of his own - that her father could barely be in the same room with her crass American beau. Or, was my insipid brother simply a perfect replication of her own jack-ass of an old man. A self-destructive way of returning to that sorry house in Lower Bockhampton where Basil always made his daughter feel small and unnecessary? For Vincent, after a fine honeymoon, did the same exact thing by relegating his newly beloved wife to the velvet curtained wings, promoting only his precious violin to center stage.

But, had she lived in a happier place during her formative years, would dear Julia still have become the commandingly gifted poet she eventually became? I firmly believe so. Those sort of resplendent skills come from a place of wonder and can not be denied. Even if you neglect to pluck them out from under that dark and foreboding bushel, or forget to regularly water them with industry, and never set them out into the graceful warmth of daylight - they still blossom. In spite of the world's callous indifference, renumeration or no, they flourish, simply because there is no other way. A thoughtful and informed voice, like that of Julia's or Aoife Coghlan's, must sometimes shout beyond life's choking constraints. Calling to be heard. Needing to be seen. Like a maple seedling defiantly rising up from between the cracks of a sidewalk, or a slender blade of grass successfully exploding into the light through a dense black sea of hardened macadam, a person's creative expression can not be inhibited, except from within. Only by denying one's own pure talents can that will to create be successfully thwarted. Thankfully, Julia had no such notions.

In point of contrast, I had really swell parents. A loving mother ... *and* a loving father, and what an often cranky and unyielding fellow I sometimes turned out to be. My road to creativity was both fully paved and well lit and yet, in my heart of hearts, Julia's clarity of expression through the use of simple words always surpassed my grand attempts at art.

Like her mother before her, dear Saoirse also chose a vicious and unworthy fellow to be her bridegroom. Richard Delaney was a perfect blending of both her grandpa Basil's incivility and papa Vincent's selfish demeanor, but without their witty yet condescending repartee. Richard, the dullard, wasn't bright enough for that. Like any venomous snake, he could only spit and curse. Again, one wonders why she'd chosen him for such an important role. Was it payback, self-flagellation, or simply a means of acting out? For my way of thinking, in each case, the price these two gifted women paid for their poor choices was far too dear. Life, as we all know, is far too short to have had to endure such flagrant assholes - especially when it's by choice and not the random circumstance of birth.

You're probably thinking about the phrase *you've made your bed, now lie in it.* I did too, but for only a moment. It's rather mean spirited don't you think - especially if you love the one involved, for it doesn't consider all the various circumstances that puts a person in that bed? Lack of financial resources, fear of being left alone in an even more dangerous world, or perhaps escaping a parents' incessant cruelties, all could place an individual in that place of ridicule.

Do women really base such enduring decisions on trivial things such as *rugged good looks* and *he's a snappy dresser* or is it simply an *I can fix this mess* kind of thing? If left to their own devices, my experience suggests that women generally do try to build things up rather than tear them down (they do tend to tear each other down a bit, but that's another story). It's most often done through a series of tender, but persistent persuasions. Like, a*re you really going to wear those pants with that shirt?* or *do you really want*

to be seen in public wearing that dreadful porkpie hat?
Gentle guidances mostly.

Men (being men) on the other hand, do so with the subtlety of hammers. In order to obtain a certain desired change in their mates, these wily fellows sometimes remark about how sexy some stranger's short skirt or itsy bitsy bikini is - which, despite their repeated attempts, never ends in a peaceful resolution. Although taking it to extremes such as: *Yes! You do look fat in that dress* would certainly put a quick end to the most tenuous of relationships.

In my case, I was always considered a "real fixer upper" - not bad enough to tear down immediately, but generally salvageable. Even at my oldest adult age, I'm proud to say, I was still considered quite *trainable.* Although, I'm convinced that the few women who deigned to love me mostly did so out of pure mercy. They would never admit it, but I'm almost certain that was predominately the case. Even in my most disguised and deluded aspects, I no doubt still appeared as though I wholeheartedly needed their love - which I most ardently did.

As with her father Vincent, Saoirse's husband Richard was a compelling and complicated man bent on holding her down and controlling every aspect of her life. As a tenured policeman, Delaney certainly had to have seen much in the world that would forever taint his view of his fellow man, sending any reserve of goodwill immediately to the trash heap. Based on this skewed logic, his fertile yet furtive imagination created various false scenarios in which his loving wife was both a practiced liar and routinely unfaithful - requiring him to physically and psychologically reprimand her at every perceived indiscretion. Saoirse was neither and deserved only his love and sincere gratefulness that she'd descended from the heavens to comfort him in his unworthiness. As you might imagine, the resulting purple bruises on my dear Saoirse's neck and shoulders made me angry. Even as ancient as I was when I first found out about all this jealous cruelty, I would've gladly risked life and limb to stop him. Fortunately, a much younger fellow was able to step in and restrain Delaney's fevered ferocity and give him a vivid taste of his own violence. While I would've thoroughly enjoyed pummeling dear Richard with my fists until they were bloody, in my own less brutal way, I was grateful for the opportunity of helping to end that sour marriage and allow my sweet dove to fly free once again.

Life sometimes offers you these tiny nuggets of redemption. They are rare and wonderful. Although, one has to have pulled his head out of his own arse just long enough to see that illuminated chance for sincere change. While I sometimes could - Richard never did.

I must also tell you about my sweet Lorraine (Cummins) Mullaney, as she too is a major player in this story. All those years alone in the Adirondack Mountains had taught her well in fending for herself. Nature was so impressed that it sided with her and had forgiven Lorraine any signs of aging. To this day, she is still a high-spirited woman who, even as she nears the age when I opted to step off the wire, displays none of my once sorry and tired ailments. She walks that same confident walk just as she did in her thirties. Has no reason yet to dye her fine russet hair. What wrinkles there are, have only gathered at the corners of her mouth - mostly as the result of too much unbridled laughter - much of which was my fault. It seems, something about me always made her giggle. I'm still not certain what it was. Maybe it was my skewed perspective on the world, or simply my overdeveloped and prevailing absurdity. She still reads voraciously without the need for glasses and can therefore talk intelligently on any subject with great authority. Her mind and memory are those of a young adult - only far less scattered.

My favorite insight by Lorraine was this thoughtful gem:

"*How different the world would be if those who chose to miss-edit the original apostles' description of Jesus had instead retained his true identity.*"

She understood the need in bending his sacred image

to better suit that of the Vatican's early European purposes... so truth be damned.

"But by all accounts, given the region of his birth, Jesus was most certainly a black, middle-eastern socialist Jew - not the pale red-bearded man he's been so often made to resemble. Based on this, Lorraine wisely wondered, *"would we have enslaved so many men of colour around this world had they been seen by us as the very likeness of God?"*

I think not.

Lorraine had never had to depend on anyone for anything, except for love. Perhaps it was her independent streak that'd kept her from marrying anyone, until I finally wore her down. Although, I immediately challenged this original supposition as being far too simplistic - deciphering any woman could never be that straightforward. Women like Lorraine were very complex creatures and therefore warranted years and years of precise hands-on investigation. That delicate and time-consuming detective work, as everyone knows, is the most interesting part of any intimate relationship.

Best of all, Lorraine literally saved my life. When my heart decided, all on its own volition, to suddenly stop pumping, she pushed and pushed and breathed life back into me. Lorraine would not be denied. That sweet taste of her lips on mine that fateful day could never be duplicated - try as I may over the years. My payment for this successful effort to reignite my heart was to finally make love to her. I'm certain that I got the best part of that deal as well.

Each day, while we were together, I attempted to show Lorraine just how much I loved her by performing a very simple act - the setting out of her morning tea. I know it's a small thing. Not a bouquet of roses or some grand gesture. Just her favorite brown ceramic mug with a fresh tea bag set inside - quietly waiting for her to wake up and pour in the hot water. It makes me sad now with the realization that when she pours that morning cup of tea, Lorraine knows that I've had nothing to do with it - not any more.

Sometimes in the dark, I can hear her call out my name.

GABRIEL!

My response is always a blend of *but darlin' I'm right here beside you* and *why am I so damn far away?*

Now that you have a little background, our story can begin. The following events all took place about fifteen years after Peter left his beloved Adirondacks, attended college, and wandered off into the wider world, making the year roughly 2005. For my own clarity, as being dead seriously clouds one's memory, I recall that there are wars being fought in both Iraq (with some questions about there actually having been any real Weapons of Mass Destruction) and Afghanistan (the actual home of the vile cowards responsible for 9/11); Hurricane Katrina, with all her intensity, attempted to wash away both Louisiana and most of southern Mississippi; dear Rosa Parks and my friends R. C. Gorman, Saul Bellows, and August

Willson will all pass away - not to mention that there are only two Beatles left in the world. Harold Pinter wins himself a Nobel Prize for Literature, and Spain will become the first country to legalize same-sex marriages. I'm sure hundreds of other just as interesting things happen as well, but you get the idea.

After our tiny wedding and wonderfully pleasant honeymoon, Lorraine and I moved into her modest house near Moose Lake. Cozy - yes, but there wasn't much room for overnight guests much less a painting studio - a truly essential requirement given my time-honored occupation. The second bedroom, her only extra space, had long been set up for giving piano lessons. The tiny one car garage had no heat and was full to the rafters with stuff.

It should be noted here that Lorraine has always been and still is a very gifted teacher. By evidence of her time with me, she is a very patient and understanding woman. To this day, a child can always be a real child in her benevolent presence.

Therefore, allowing space for her baby grand piano was every bit as important as my having a room to set up an easel. So our first joint adventure as a married couple was to begin looking for a much larger home - a chore that I immediately left in Lorraine's capable hands. My world at that time was still filled with back-to-back commercial art commissions, requiring me to spend much too much time traveling and in New York City.

"Don't work so very hard," Lorraine would lovingly caution. "After your little event back there at Atwell's cabin, the doctors want you to relax more."

"I blame my brother Vincent for all that heart attack nonsense… ."

"Yes. Vincent certainly knows how to raise your blood pressure."

"It's like he knows where the coronary on and off switch is."

"All the same, my dearest, you have got to slow down… ."

"I've only got so much time," I'd reply knowingly, having already felt the chilled and unshakable presence of the reaper. "There's still so much for me to do."

"I know," she would purr with compassionate understanding, fully aware that I'd silently push through the pain should my chest ever again begin to tighten.

"There's so much cued up within my mind's eye… ."

"But, what about your heart?"

"Not to worry. It still loves you... and always will."

After she kissed me sweetly, I added, "I'm more worried about my eyes. The darkness comes more and more frequently now and I just need to get all those compositions out on canvas, before... ."

"They are such splendid eyes," Lorraine reflected, as she tilted her head slightly to the left comparing my stale irises to that of the actual flowers."

Right there, in that moment while studying her face as she admired mine, another necessary portrait joined the pending cue.

"Not to worry my love. I'd see your sweet face and be able to paint it even if my eyes were sewn shut."

Just as I knew she would, Lorraine found us a fine 1860's Queen Anne Victorian in the sleepy village of Nutting, New York - not far from either the Adirondacks or the Mohawk River. From there, the drive down to Redden to see my son Eugene and his wife Sile would take less than an hour and a half (as the crow flies).

Standing alongside her on the tree shaded sidewalk, looking up at Lorraine's fortuitous find, there was a soft glow of achievement surrounding her gentle countenance. The place would be perfect for us. Seeing her that way convinced me that I could actually make her happy - which was really all I wanted to accomplish.

The house was located on Canal Avenue at the intersection of five roads, kind of like the five-points section in Lower Manhattan. Our well established neighborhood was bounded to the west by Centre Street, to the east by Bowery Boulevard and the substantially tree lined Parkrow Place to the south.

The house itself was both grey-green on the first floor and chiffon yellow above, with cream-coloured gingerbread all about. The Mansard roof and trim were both brick red and Hooker's green depending on the story level. Colour wise I couldn't imagine changing a thing. It was as though I had chosen the tints and hues myself in a previous life.

Lorraine's miraculous find also featured a steeply pitched roof, a front-facing gable, and a full-width front porch - which provided plenty of practical exterior room for waving to neighbors and drinking our morning tea together. There was also a second entrance off the side porch, which would allow her piano students (should there be any) to enter and leave the house without interrupting our little family. The den beyond that side door was a perfect place to plant her baby grand. Best of all, it had a fully-windowed turret on the northern side of the house. Northern light my friends! A perfect place for my studio! It was the very feature that drew her in when she saw the Canal Street house's picture in the realtor's dream book.

To celebrate our closing on the house, we retreated to that very turret, shed our clothes, and made love right there in the afternoon sun. That celestial warmth and her soft whispers of joy still linger in my mind. How, with such pure exuberance, could they not extend beyond the grave and follow me to this place? Along with breathing, having sex with Lorraine is one of the few things that I miss now "that I'm supposedly *with* the angels".

We had five good years on Canal Avenue. Lorraine did choose to teach piano, but only occasionally, while I worked my pallet knife on a succession of fairly successful canvases - despite my ever advancing macular degeneration. Oddly, now that I don't need my eyes to see, that ignominious disease is completely gone.

Along with these renewed visual powers of mine, I can sometimes see right inside another man's heart. Something that would have been quite useful back while I was alive and trying to buy a used car. Often though, the effect is rather horrifying. Whenever I'm forced to see the stark hypocrisy of truth being so carefully disguised by practiced expression - especially in those friendly countenances where I never once imagined that any false acceptance ever existed - I'm appalled. Thankfully, those exasperating moments of despair are easily tempered by simply looking into the soul of a child - innocence being such a resplendent pick-me-up. But you don't have to be dead like me to enjoy that special tonic. Just stop whatever it is that you're doing and look around - really look, and listen for a wee giggle.

Speaking of listening, I must say that hearing Lorraine's neophyte keyboardists learning their instrument down below my turret certainly added to my momentary methodology. If a lad was punishing the ivories with far too many errant notes, the pattern of my brushstrokes followed suit - tending to be choppy and staying well outside the lines. On the other hand, if a lassie was point-on and her melody was grand, so too was my overall effort.

Listening to music is the only way that I could work. Music, in its definable rhythms and beats, strips away everything else and allows the composition to come clearly through the visual haze. My interests were always eclectic - never remaining in one style for very long, but fluctuating along with mood and sudden desire. So... a well-intentioned child pummeling a baby grand piano fit in well, as you never knew if they'd practiced, wanted to be there at all, or loved the act of creation as much as you did. Unfortunately, the latter were very few in number, but certainly cherished in their pure rarity of purpose.

Did Lorraine have any Diana Kralls or Carole Kings amongst her pupils? Some. There were five or six students who went on to study music in college. A few of them even became music teachers themselves - spreading her teachings like mellifluous spores across the sonic countryside. One became a traveling troubadour - roaming about the continent like some hobo balladeer. Most though, took what she taught them and applied it to the calming of their daily lives. Music, you'll agree, is less tricky to get than heroin, and is far easier on the liver than whiskey. Sitting at a piano, working the keys, can surely transform one's day from sheer anxiety to that of sudden serenity upon the first note - whether that note be on pitch or not. Only one of her students went into show business. We heard that he got nominated for a Golden Globe, but unfortunately, he lost out to Mick Jagger and Dave Stewart that year.

With us now living in Nutting, Lorraine's old house near Moose Lake would have to be dealt with.

Sell it? No. Too many good memories for that.

Rent it? Don't really want to, what with having to deal with a random series of demanding strangers and such living there.

Rent it seasonally? No. Exuberant and tactless tourists can do a number on a place if they chose to over celebrate - which is after all their default setting.

Shutter it and simply forget about it? No. Lorraine respected the house far too much for that. She'd enjoyed fixing the roof and replacing the siding by her own hand, as it was her way of giving back for a safe and dry place to live.

There was also a fifth option that we didn't realize we had until the letter from Saoirse arrived.

It turned out that our darling niece needed a quiet place to recuperate from knee surgery (a bicycle accident we were told), not to mention that her sixth floor apartment in Queens no longer had a working elevator. Plus, she also wanted a quiet place to finish her latest book - which I completely understood, having done a very similar thing a few years before myself at Atwell's cabin.

Since publishing that splendid collection of her mother Julia's poems alongside my early drawings, Saoirse had become a very desired biographer. Her timely 2003 biography of Pulitzer Prize winning cartoonist Bill Mauldin (a good friend of mine since World War II) came out just after his death and was critically praised. That success - as often happens when talent and tenaciousness are in sweet cohabitation - led to other fine works such as *Ogdred Weary: The Life of Edward Corey; Among Gnomes and Trolls* about Swedish illustrator John Bauer; and *Impressions of Shinnecock* about landscape painter William Merritt Chase. She was rather tight-lipped regarding the subject of her latest work, but that's understandable, given how transient a writing project can be at the very beginning, so we didn't press her for details.

Lorraine's idea was to simply give Saoirse the property and let her to do with it as she willed. Live in it. Which was her favorite plan for our niece. Renting it or selling it were likely the best bet if she needed the money. In my wife's mind, the kind act of giving the property away removed her from any further claim the premises had over her. She'd done her very best to maintain the house against the ravages of weather and time as just compensation for the house having looked after her. Now it would be Saoirse's responsibility.

Her letter had asked if she could come and stay with us mid-month, which worked out fine for Lorraine and me. There was an exhibit opening soon requiring my attendance on the 10th, so anytime after that was fine. When we finished the letter, we looked at each other and smiled. It would be grand to see our dear Saoirse again.

Across the country, in a sweeping desert plane, Peter was busy bracing his easel against the pummeling wind and scouring tumbleweeds. The landscape he was intending to paint was putting up a fight - throwing everything it had at his canvas like a fierce gale against a trembling sail. Obviously, being a shy vista, it didn't want its soul being so capriciously captured. The Santa Fe sun was doing its fair share as well - spearing steaming heat rays like firebrand javelins all around him. When his freshly stretched canvas blew away for the fifth time, rolling on its corners like a silver-dollar across the dunes, he decided to call it a day.

"Maybe the wind will blow itself out tonight and I'll get another chance tomorrow," he thought with youthful optimism, but he knew the truth. When the El Niño winds started to blow like this they could do so in continuous spans of seven years.

"How is that Georgia O'Keeffe managed to paint here," he wondered aloud as he packed up his gear. "I know... she took her collected flowers and bones back to the quiet of her studio, which is what I would do if I could move those distant mesas."

His time in New Mexico was coming to an end. The temp-job he'd gotten at The New Mexico Museum of Art in Santa Fe would be over soon. Once he finished assisting with the hanging of their final show of the season he'd be on an eastbound train. The exhibition in the Laguna Gallery was a re-creation of the museum's 1917 inaugural exhibition - which included paintings by New York transplant and superb urban painter George Bellows (*Tesuque Pueblo*), local scenic painter Cordelia Wilson (*A Mexican House*) and the exceptional landscape painter Leon Kroll (*Santa Fe Hills*).

Leon Kroll's inclusion was what initially drew Peter to the project. He'd first seen the Eastern artist's work in a retrospective exhibition at the Byrdcliffe Art Colony not far from the city of Redden in Woodstock, New York. A very young Kroll had studied at the colony himself in 1906, just before going off to study in Europe. Kroll's lush brushwork, rousing compositions, and vivid palette mirrored that of Peter's own artistic approach. Influenced by Matisse and Georges Braque of the Fauvist Movement, Kroll (and now Peter) used his paint directly from the tube, never mixing beforehand. The final effect was not unlike that of Vincent Van Gogh. Traveling here allowed Peter to see the inspiration for both Kroll's and Bellow's New Mexican landscapes first hand.

It surprised Peter how the natural colours of New Mexico were so very different from those he'd become accustomed to in upstate New York. The unexpected blends had changed his mind's pallet forever. The lush blues, greens, and umbers of the eastern forests were now forever replaced by the faded ochers and dull carmines of the expansive west. On his way across country, Peter could tell with complete certainty where New Mexico ended and the Arizona border began simply by noticing the end of a muted salmon-coloured fault line running through the Zuni Mountains.

When Peter entered the Laguna gallery, Lisbeth Santoro, the exhibit's curator, was waiting for him. Her dark hair and deep olive skin were another change. Before meeting her, he'd always dreamt about Irish girls - mostly because of that one in particular named Saoirse who'd so thoroughly entranced our dear Peter in his youth. Lisbeth walked differently too. There was a dancer's cadence to her sybaritic stride that always seemed to capture a man's attention.

There were flaws as well - for whenever she could fit it in the conversation, Lisbeth would remind Peter that she was the grandniece of famed Italian painter Rubens Santoro. The mandolin playing landscape painter from Calabria (the toe of Italy's boot), who had been well respected in his time and according to her, very well collected.

"His realism always makes me want to visit Naples," she would say, regarding her distant uncle's work. "He was a master of composition and light."

"You should go to Naples," Peter would reply - hoping Lisbeth would go tomorrow and give him some peace. Something about her always clouded his thinking while she was near - making it very hard to concentrate on more mundane matters. In fact, Rory, one of his less sophisticated fellow workers, often forgot to breathe whenever she strolled by.

"Wouldn't you miss me?" Lisbeth whispered, hoping that Peter would.

"I'd rather you fulfilled a dream," he replied, knowing full well that any entanglement between the two of them was doomed to fail.

"Yes! But I have dreams that you can help me fulfill right here - and now."

There was a sparkle in her eye that he couldn't ignore. Since he'd arrived at the gallery two months ago, the beautiful and enticing Ms. Santoro had been relentlessly pursuing him. She liked his granite shoulders and sinewy forearms, but most of all, his polite manner - old worldly really - which she found wonderfully refreshing in today's often crass society.

He reminded her of what traveling artists must have been like during her Great Great Uncle's day.

"Shall we hang the Robert Henri pieces today?" he asked, hoping to change the subject. "There's got to be at least fourteen of them?"

"The crew began unpacking them last night," Lisbeth replied feeling a bit neglected. "They should be ready to install later this afternoon."

"Then, how about I buy you some lunch?" Peter offered, feeling guilty. He couldn't help being so damn handsome. Wait... that's an editorial bias on my part. The truth is... Peter liked Lisbeth, but he knew that he'd be leaving soon. There'd been a letter from the Adirondacks calling him eastward. Peter felt no need in hurrying to do so. Mostly because that part of the world hadn't been his home for more than half his life, and his old Newton's Corners' neighbor's sad correspondence had told him that his father was already dead and buried.

You'd think, after placing such a terrible strain on the world's overall well-being for so many wretched decades, I would've noticed the exact moment of Atwell's death, but unlike the way they lowered the lights on Broadway for Harold Pinter, Elaine Stritch, or Mike Nichols, not even a single 25 watt bulb dimmed at his passing.

When Peter considered the death of his father, the idea of his being gone forever and ever was more complicated than he'd expected. Yes. Begrudgingly, he loved Atwell, like any faithful son should love his father, but he completely disliked the man that he grew to know. Where Atwell could've chosen to make things more pleasant around the cabin after Peter's mother's death, his father chose to stifle any joyful temptations and embraced only rampant cynicism instead. Like any young lad, Peter was hurting. Couldn't his old man see it?! He loved his mother deeply. She'd been the bright sustaining beam that so consistently held their family upright into the light. With her sudden disappearance from the Earth, unrelenting darkness returned with interest, and nothing spewing from Atwell's terse lips saw the good in anything or anyone ever again. If our youthful Peter had been a hothouse flower, instead of a loving and impressionable boy, the greenhouse that he now found himself in was tightly shuttered by cold pessimism and dull murkiness, leaving him to be submersed in his father's pure fatalistic manure - instead of an invigorating bath poured of sunlight.

"So... Can I take you to lunch?" Peter asked Lisbeth again in the gallery's foyer later that morning. He was looking forward to a bit of pleasurable distraction.

"Yes! Please!" Her excited reply left Lisbeth feeling a little emotionally exposed. She hadn't meant to blurt out her answer so emphatically.

"Wonderful," Peter replied, giving her his warmest smile. "I've just got those three Gerald Cassidy paintings to uncrate... ."

"That shouldn't take you too long. Shall we meet out in front of the gallery at 11:50?"

"Perfect."

Peter couldn't help but watch Lisbeth as she strolled away. Neither could any of the other working folks assembled in the gallery that morning - man or woman. She just had that kind of walk.

The first of the three Cassidy paintings needed no un-crating. *Cui Bono* had been made a gift of the artist to the museum nearly eighty-eight years ago. The painting's latin title means "to whose profit?" Today that phrase is considered a key forensic question: *finding out who has a motive to commit a specific crime.* Detectives always need to decide that important distinction before they can decide how to proceed with any investigation. Cassidy's intention was much less criminal. He simply wanted to reinforce the idea of native people as being noble. To that end, the central figure in his painting is shown wearing what resembles a white Romanesque toga. The statuesque fellow could be a Roman Senator standing there with such dignity. Cassidy's idealized Navajo man was a symbol, Peter'd been told, created to represent a prolonged and peaceful civilization whose enduring roots extend deep into the soil - even now - having started from the very beginning of time.

Gerald Cassidy was another transplanted easterner - born in Kentucky, raised in Ohio, and educated in New York. Like many others in his day, it was a serious illness that'd brought him to the health clinics of Albuquerque - where, from then on, the people and vistas of New Mexico would forever hold his creative Art Deco imagination. Peter completely understood how the discovery of a western pallet could forever influence a man and his art. It had done so to him as well.

As Peter's crew carefully carried the nearly four foot by eight foot framed canvas across the wide Laguna Gallery, he studied the faded yellow brush strokes of Cassidy's adobe mud brick wall and stone floor. Then he surveyed the visual cluster of the adobe homes set just off-center that the artist had left to bake in the hot morning sun. The distant green sky and blue patterned hills awakened the landscape painter in him - making Peter wish he'd thought of the composition first. Finally, he noticed that the central figure's eyes had the same mystical yet human quality as does da Vinci's enigmatic *Mona Lisa*.

All the while, as they carefully hung the giant portrait, Peter looked over at the Navajo Senator, waiting for him to whisper whatever that thought was that he'd held so silently for nearly ninety years. If he spoke, Peter didn't hear it.

Just before noon, Peter found himself standing in the bright sunlight on Lincoln Avenue. The same radiant glow that Gerald Cassidy had so competently captured in *Cui Bono* shone all around him. Light, he knew, was timeless.

Soon Lisbeth was standing beside him, just as she'd promised. He smiled as she deftly slipped her hand inside his elbow. The unexpected electricity of her touch beguiled him.

"Where should we go?" There was a bright carefree tone to Peter's question.

"The Plaza Cafe is just up the street," Lisbeth suggested. "How about we go there?"

"Why not? I could sure go for some of their Green Chile Meatloaf right about now."

"Then that's where we'll go."

Slowly, they walked arm-in-arm down the covered walkway, stopping only briefly to look into the Trading Company's windows. There was a pair of leather boots on display there that Lisbeth knew she'd probably be looking at more closely after work. Life, she'd learned early, sometimes required the occasional gift, even if that bright offering was self-generated.

Surprisingly, when they got to the cafe, there was a man sitting on the red bench outside waiting for them. There was an agitated look in his eyes that immediately caught Peter's attention.

"Where have you been Lisbeth?" the stranger asked angrily. "I've been sitting here almost seven minutes already."

"Oh, hello," Lisbeth happily greeted the man, choosing to overlook his seemingly contemptible attitude. "Issac Lemkin, this is my friend Peter. He'll be joining us for lunch."

Suddenly, Peter realized that Lisbeth's choice of restaurants wasn't as capricious as it'd originally sounded. She already had a lunch date meeting her here.

"And...why would *he* be doing that?" Issac harshly replied showing little concern for poor Peter's feelings.

"He's asked me to lunch, and I've accepted."

"But I asked you first!"

"I'm sure the cafe has plenty of food for everyone," Peter interrupted, as he offered to shake hands with the surly man.

Issac chose to ignore the friendly gesture and abruptly turned and walked into the restaurant. Lisbeth and Peter followed - each giving the other a knowing smile. Obviously, Issac was bright enough to see that he'd just become the third wheel.

The Plaza Cafe is a 1950's Retro eatery, with a high white square-patterned tin ceiling, black and white checked tile floor, chrome trimmed tables, and a half-dozen wide red vinyl booths. A chrome bar with red circular stools still runs the full length on its right side. The dark wooden chairs scattered about are the substantial kind, like the ones found in courthouses and lawyer's offices.

"Two cups of coffee and a tea, please Mrs. Patmore," Lisbeth said to her favorite waitress, as the trio slipped into a booth. No matter the number of patrons, the veteran waitress would need no pad or pencil, as her memory always caught every detail. "I've guessed right haven't I boys?" Lisbeth asked gaily. She was thoroughly enjoying the sudden competitive nature of this gathering.

"*I very much like being the prize,*" she thought to herself.

"Indeed Ezbeth," Issac replied, cleverly slipping in his nickname for her, hoping the annoying interloper would see that he already had a claim on this woman. "I do love the coffee here."

Given his rather neanderthalish appearance, archeologists might have chosen to use Issac Lemkin as the basis for one of their more fanciful museum mannequins. His overly-large cranium was most certainly well stuffed with knowledge, having matriculated from Rutger's University would've seen to that. Issac's dark sunken eyes maintained a constant squint, no doubt from having read too many textbooks, while his wide flat nose held a kind of pre-sneeze posture, most likely from decades of exposure to law library dust. The receding hairline he'd inherited from his father was successfully balanced by a full, yet well-trimmed black beard. The word handsome could be used, but only loosely, to describe him. When people saw Issac arm-in-arm with a lady-friend, he was the guy who proved the old theory that woman don't always go by looks when choosing a mate. Sometimes a strong personality or fine humor could tip the scale in a suitor's favour. Unfortunately, sullen Issac could boast neither of those qualities.

The trio grew silent as Issac sat quietly, looking longingly at Lisbeth's face. She felt the heat of his uninterrupted gaze, and not knowing what to do, simply endured its sad fervency.

Issac so wanted to ask her why the sudden interloper. What had he done to disappoint? Surely, their first two dates had gone well enough - or at least he thought so. After all, he'd allowed her to take him 'disco' dancing, and then to see a rather liberal-leaning film called *Good Bye Lenin!* together. Christ, he'd already been able to garner the briefest of goodnight kisses.

"So Issac. What fills your cheery days here in Santa Fe - when you're not in some cafe drinkin' coffee?" Peter asked, breaking the spell, only slightly interested in actually hearing this brusque man's answer.

"I'm a lawyer," Issac replied with great pride.

"Couldn't you tell," Lisbeth interrupted, "by simply observing his brilliant white shirt, Phi Alpha Delta necktie, and splendid three-piece suit?"

"Really? By his gloomy demeanor, I thought Lemkin here was some kind of disgruntled undertaker," Peter thought to himself, before replying, "Yes. That explains quite a lot actually, especially, why in all this confounded heat, the man is so fully dressed."

"I've just come from the courthouse... ."

"Ah! Then you'll just have to pardon my cargo shorts and hightop sneakers - but wait, my shirt does have a collar."

"It really is a fine suit Isaac and so very professional looking." Lisbeth's compliment was gratefully received. He appreciated her understanding that a man likes to dress nicely too. "But I'm also enjoying those pretty pink knees," Lisbeth teased, leading Peter to blush a bit.

From the outside, you'd think that this was a classic love triangle, but it really wasn't. Lisbeth only felt sympathy for the overly obsessed and rather lonely attorney - while she liked Peter quite a lot. Peter liked Lisbeth a lot too, and given their interaction so far, immediately disliked Issac's overt pretentiousness.

Waiting seven minutes - really?

Issac may have pretended an affection for Lisbeth, but in Peter's mind, the man loved himself far too much to allow anyone else into his tiny little heart. It was most likely that Issac's mommy-dearest thought he should be married by now and Lisbeth was the best option for achieving that modest goal - ASAP.

"I'm guessin' corporate law," Peter offered with a wry wink. "You don't look like a civil rights kind of guy to me. If you were, you'd be dressed in wool tweeds with leather elbow-patches... ."

"Mergers and acquisitions are just as important," Issac replied, feeling annoyed at the near-snub. "How could our great nation have grown to such prominence without them?"

"Sure they're important," Peter offered flatly as he silently thought, *"just ask any of the indigenous folks around here - who were gullible enough to sign governmental treaties - what their thoughts regarding the mergers and acquisitions are."*

"I'm also involved with cilvil rights issues," Issac countered. "Companies have first amendment rights too you know. Someday the Supreme Court will support such a crucial ruling."

Turns out that old Issac was right. In 2010, *Corporate Personhood* becomes a reality - allowing businesses to make vast political expenditures under the First Amendment, just like us *natural* blood and guts folks. What could go wrong there?

"And you? What is it that you do?" Isaac's condescension was palpable. "Let me guess," he began, placing a thumb on his chin as he leaned back on his chair. "With all that long hair and that faded chambray shirt,... you're some sort of musician - am I right?"

"I'll take that as a compliment. But no... I'm an artist - landscapes mostly," Peter replied. His pride in his chosen profession was evident too.

"What the hell does that mean - an artist?"

"It is what it is. You're a lawyer, she's a waitress, and I'm an artist!"

"Be nice boys," Lisbeth warned, although she was clearly enjoying the floorshow. There was heat growing between these two men that was suddenly fueling her own growing ardor.

"But the law is an important thing. A monumental thing." Isaac's chest was puffing out like some fully tufted Tom-turkey. "It's what our great nation is built upon. No civilization can exist without the rule of law. In its purest form, it's the booming voice of justice for everyone all around the world - rich or poor. You, as a mere artist, can only speak to those few imbeciles who, lured in by free cheese and wine, are dull enough to be willing to listen."

"It's more than that and you know it."

Sorry, but I must interject a comment here. Despite what our lawyer friend firmly believes, *"Civilizations are not remembered by their business people, their bankers or lawyers. They're remembered by the arts,"* my friend and Art entrepreneur Eli Broad once told to me. Just look back at ancient Egypt for an example. We remember the pyramids and the Sphinx far more easily than any of their indisputable laws.

"Art, as far as I'm concerned," Issac continued, "is just pretty little pictures painted at pretty little seaside resorts by pretty little insignificant so-and-so's. It's what people do in their retirement simply to kill time, while others stay on the front lines, like me, and continue to do society's real work... ."

"Sometimes," Peter half agreed thinking of his not-so-very-talented cousin Frank - the Cape Cod summer tourist painter. "But it's also that lovely three-pieced suit you're so proud of wearing. Some dimwitted artist had to design that bag of pin-striped cloth so that you'd look like a human being rather than some simian creature who'd escaped from the zoo - not to mention her having designed that fine Cartier watch on your wrist."

"Don't start with all that designer nonsense... ."

"It's not nonsense," Lisbeth chimed in. "Who do you think designed that baby-blue Porsche that you're so fond of driving around in or that swanky adobe bungalow that you'll definitely be going home *alone* to tonight?"

"I'm so tired of you artsy-fartsy types, making out like you're so damn insightful. I'll have you know, it took me seven years of study at Rutgers to get where I am today." It was important that he should name his prestigious university so that this silly artist fellow could, by vivid contrast, recognize his absolute comparative diminutiveness.

"I don't think your professors brightened enough of your horizons there my friend," Peter replied, suddenly feeling rather sorry for this obviously near-sighted man. Lemkin was so full of himself that he couldn't allow for anyone else to have accomplished anything. "If you'd bothered to have taken the hour and a half ride down to Camden, you'd have seen that Rutgers has a fully functioning art department too. Obviously, the University understands the importance of both fields of study."

"Next you'll be bringing up Modern Art. What a confounded lie that is."

"Lie?"

"Yes. It's all so unintelligible," Issac countered. "Simply the creation of some art dealer's moronic vision of what's supposedly cool and trendy. Christ! I remember reading about a painter who used urine on his canvases and another who employed powdered elephant dung."

"That would be Andy Warhol and Chris Ofili - both rather respected artists in their time.

"Urine and feces. Really?"

"It's their artistic vision... ."

"Warhol just proves my point" Issac sneered. "Nothing he ever did was original. He simply stole whole images from others, smeared some ink over them and called it art. If it wasn't for some gaggle of colluding art dealers and simple-minded critics, he'd have vanished long before attaining his fleeting fifteen minutes of fame."

"OK. Not everybody likes poor Andy," Peter half-agreed. "Just like after defending that Brentwood killer O. J. Simpson, not everybody's so crazy about Robert Kardashian."

"That kind of art is a lie because it's been conjured up... ."

"Even if I agreed with that flawed logic," Peter replied, again remembering artist and critique Marcel Duchamp who, like Lemkin, questioned the very idea of Art, the adoration of which he found quite unnecessary. "It still doesn't rule out realism (which Duchamp called 'retinal art' because it was only concerned with beauty and not down-and-dirty reality)."

"Why do I need an artist to capture an existing view, when even back in 1888 a Kodak box camera could easily do just that - without all the hype and it only cost a dollar?"

"Sure, if you only wanted it in black and white."

"They make colour film now too - don't they?!"

"Yeah. But by using a camera, it's no different than wielding a brush to record that view. Box camera or no, it's still an artist's tool."

"It's pushing a button for Christ sake. Nothing more."

"Ansel Adams might disagree with your argument counselor," Peter replied. "There's still composition, lighting, and texture to be considered... ."

"Does that disdain for art also include me Isaac?" Lisbeth wanted to know.

"No Ezbeth," Isaac emphatically replied, clearly hating being cross-examined from all sides. "I'll allow you as the sole exception. I imagine it takes a lot of schooling to become a curator - even if it's only an *art* curator."

"Finish your coffee then, and go," Lisbeth ordered. "I'll not dine with a man who doesn't respect what I do."

"But Ezbeth?!"

"Mrs. Patmore, we're ready to order now," Lisbeth called out ignoring Isaac's pitiful plea for leniency. "It'll be lunch for two, our solicitor friend here can't stay and will be leaving."

"Bye bye Isaac," Peter called out as the lawyer got up to go. "And... just so you know,... some dimwitted artist also designed those lovely Florsheim shoes that you're wearing, as well as the ceramic tile that they're even now walking out on - not to mention that splendid oak door you'll be so permanently leaving through... ."

I heard Lemkin's bitter reply, and it's not worth repeating in mixed company.

It should be noted here that there could still be a happy future for poor Issac, if only he allowed himself the freedom. Writer Studs Terkel (who studied law for three years in Chicago), Russian abstract painter Wassily Kandinsky (a law lecturer until he was 30), and even my favorite French Impressionist painter Henri Matisse (once a court administrator and the artist that caused Duchamp to coin the phrase 'retinal art') all had embraced the law before turning to the joy of creating art.

"I'm guessing your friend Isaac dislikes music as much as he hates art," Peter offered when they were finally alone.

"I don't think Isaac understands the inherent freedom in either of them," Lisbeth replied after some consideration. "His kind of law is pretty black and white - made up of mostly numbers and critical clauses with little or no room for life's subtleties. I guess in his mind, art and music are far too chaotic."

"Yeah. But that's what so great about 'em," Peter enthusiastically replied. "For me, art *is* music. Its melodious beats and rests are the same as using short or long brushstrokes. Music's rising or falling arpeggios and brisk allegros can be seen in the very vibrancy or subtlety of the colours. For me, they are both truly magical."

"I'm sure that Issac sees the law as magical too."

"Maybe. Although, I'm not sure his mind works within the mystical realm."

"He does have very singular interests," Lisbeth replied. "I'm not sure why he's been pursuing me. Unlike you and I, Issac and I have so very little to talk about. I only agreed to meet him for lunch today, so he'd stop asking."

"Why?! Have you looked in the mirror lately? You're a knock-out."

"Thanks," Lisbeth replied demurely. "If I'm so beautiful, then why haven't you asked me to model for you?"

"I'm a landscape painter... remember?"

"What!? This body isn't landscape enough for you?"

Given clear permission, Peter stopped and looked at Lisbeth's figure, not as an emboldened lover, but with a keen artist's eye. Her lines and curves were in point of fact both delicate and bold - like a warm summer hillside bathed in the late afternoon sun.

"Well!?"

"Yes. I could certainly paint your portrait."

"Good," Lisbeth whispered. "How about after lunch, we put off hanging those Robert Henri paintings for a few hours and I sit for you?"

"Sounds like an inspired plan. Should we get some dessert to go?"

"Let's hold off on dessert," she replied, "and wait and see what treats we can find elsewhere."

When they arrived at Peter's apartment, he took a few quick moments to tidy up the place before allowing his unexpected guest to enter. Lisbeth, quietly amused, lingered by the front door, waiting for the all clear. She was enjoying watching Peter as he moved about the room. An approachable Adonis indeed.

"Come on in and make yourself comfortable."

"Nice apartment," Lisbeth offered as she finally stepped through the doorway. "Not much furniture though."

"There's just enough - one table, one chair, one rug... ."

"And one bed?" she asked hopefully.

"No. There's two of those actually. One in each bedroom."

"Where's your easel?"

"There - in the back bedroom."

Lisbeth sauntered across the room, took Peter's hand and led him into the makeshift studio. Being a dutiful lad, he followed her without resistance.

"Let me set up a bit, " Peter mumbled as he grabbed the elusive blank canvas that had earlier tried to run away from him in the desert and set it with a thump onto the easel.

Portraits weren't really Peter's thing, as they often required much impromptu manipulating of their elements in order to make a pleasing composition. Figure staging for balance and weight; dramatic lighting to accentuate or downplay a particular facial feature; the enhancement of various textures (say in fabrics or stuccoed walls), all played a vibrant role. In a landscape, nature does all that heavy lifting. All Peter is required to do is recognize the composition and faithfully record it.

"Where should I be?"

Looking about the room for a good horizontal background, Peter anxiously suggested that Lisbeth sit down on the bed - that way there would be a series of wide windows behind her, offering some nice landscape elements to the composition. He was nervous about proposing that specific location, as he didn't want to seem too *suggestive*. Lisbeth had no such qualms and did just as she was told - except, when she got to his bed, she began to remover her blouse.

"Could you please help me with these buttons?" she asked without reserve.

Again, Peter, being a dutiful lad, assisted her with full appreciation of her scintillating request.

"And my bra?"

"Certainly... ."

"You were intending this to be a nude portrait, were you not?" she asked him. The look in her eye told him clearly what she intended.

"Most definitely," Peter agreed, rather breathlessly. "If that's what you'd prefer. We really are a full service studio."

"What I'd prefer is that you be naked as well." Her expression was playful, yet serious. "A *nude* portrait could certainly be so defined if the artist himself were naked at the time he painted it, could it not?"

"I couldn't agree with you more," Peter replied as he deftly continued unbuttoning her blouse.

As they laid together side-by-side after their carnal gymnastics, with Lisbeth's eyes sleepy from pleasure, Peter looked over her body one more time. The afternoon sun was filling the apartment with white hot light pushing all of her gentle hues into sharp contrast. That previously fierce El Niño wind he'd so recently maligned was more playful now, calmly pushing the lace curtains around with its now whispered breath. She certainly wasn't Rubenesque, but rather more Gauguinesque in her naturalness. The arc of her supple hip was a gentle slope and thoroughly captured his imagination. In one direction it ran lithely down her long graceful thigh, ending at her shapely ankle and in the other, beyond her taught belly, drowsy ribs, and ebullient breasts, up to her splendid slender neck. No brush on canvas could ever capture such a sumptuous image. Memory. Only the memory of her graciousness would adequately preserve this moment beyond these silent adobe walls.

Memory would have to do, for even with a full night of activity, that once errant canvas never got used.

Their walk back to the gallery was slow and deliberate, as neither of them wanted to end their first night together. Again, they walked arm-in-arm down the covered walkway, only this time with the conjoined warmth of a most pleasant memory. Despite El Nino's occasional blustering gusts, the night breeze was cooler and less ferocious, allowing the dry plants along the sidewalk's edge to rustle intermittently, like waves lapping at a dock. With the sun just having dipped below the horizon, the ambient light around them now had a faded burnt orange glow to it. It was so delightful that they prayed the city's street lights would fail to ignite and not spoil the moment.

They did not speak, or at least I couldn't hear what they were saying. In truth, I think their conversations were all internal, spoken only to themselves, but regarding the other's feelings. Peter, she was certain, wasn't sure that he liked what'd seemed like a one-night-stand. He'd want more. Much more. Lisbeth silently agreed with his assessment, but unlike Peter, she knew full well that they'd make love many more times. A woman always knows these things, while a man can only remain hopeful.

On the steps of the gallery, Lisbeth pulled Peter close and kissed him. It wasn't a dutiful goodbye kiss, or a pleasantry-laden thank you kiss, or even a playful smooch. It was a formal point of punctuation stating her full intentions. She definitely wanted more lovin' too. His unmistakable and grateful reply was in the commanding way he returned that singular kiss.

Once inside, Lisbeth walked off across the gallery, fully aware that Peter would be closely watching her. Her stroll was one of practiced elegance, clearly meant to entice. As the rhythm of his breathing grew shorter and shorter, he wasn't sure that he'd be able to watch her climb the stairs and remain fully conscious. He did though... and I'm so very proud of his stamina in the face of such wondrous ankles and calves.

Later, when he was home alone, Peter looked about the apartment and began taking stock of what would have to be packed and what would have to be discarded. He couldn't afford to ship anything big, so any furniture that wasn't the landlady's soon would be hers. Of course his easel, favorite painting gear, as well as the few canvases he'd been able to paint would have to somehow find their way east. Maybe he could get a loan or borrow some cash. One thing he couldn't leave behind though was the framed print that I'd given him upon his graduation from Wainwright. It was a landscape of course, a work by one of his favorite painters: Frederic Edwin Church. The work, dated 1878, was called *Landscape in the Adirondacks*. It is a dynamic vision, offering visual hope with the new dawn. There's a canoe on the water, distant tyrian mountains, and it always reminded him of summers spent rowing on Rollins Pond. His having seen its reproduction in a school book had been the inspiration for his own first successful composition - the modest painting of the view outside his bedroom window that I not only helped him visualize, but create.

I'm going to have to sell my Minolta, Peter thought to himself. *Otherwise I'm not going to be able to ship anything of importance to New York.*

He got $150 for the camera. Just enough for shipping.

As Peter laid there alone in bed, his head spinning with both the dazzling thoughts of Lisbeth and the coming punishment of having to go home, he fought for serenity. With closed eyes, he concentrated on the single sound of a distant train whistle. It was the mournful call from one lonely iron-horse to another. As the engine's plaintive plea slipped softly into the night, he finally found a measure of peace.

Sixteen days later, when Peter's east bound train pulled into the Santa Fe Depot, Lisbeth Santoro was not there standing on the platform to see him off. For reasons all her own, they had said their goodbyes the night before, allowing Peter to revisit her soft vistas and sweeping landscapes one last time. He'd be in Lamy, New Mexico long before she even woke up.

Would she have allowed herself to follow him east? No. She'd worked far too hard to establish herself here. Santa Fe, and especially Taos, were havens for the arts and she simply couldn't leave. Sure, New York City was an art mecca too, but she already knew this particular world so intimately. A long distance romance? Again no. She attempted that untenable feat once before. Tumbleweeds would have a far better chance at keeping love alive while being two thousand miles apart.

Lisbeth was right. Lovers need to touch one another and it should happen more often than not. Not necessarily in a sexual way, but in a passive, spur of the moment kind of thing. Taking Lorraine into my arms as we passed each other in the hallway and dancing her through the kitchen only made our love deeper. You'd have to agree, that most long distant love affairs suffer greatly from a lack of spontaneity. The precise planning necessary to navigate through a swirling maze of different time zones, overlapping schedules, and varying sleep cycles can easily strip away all the fun from such a venture. And... it might be my advanced age speaking here, or my not having yet experienced the pleasures of "online-video chatting", but phone sex, for me, is just another form of lonely masturbation.

In truth, in this situation, and many more just like it before choosing to finally settle down, Lisbeth - always remaining in full control - greatly preferred the ephemeral amusement of sex to the heavy-lifting of everyday intimacy found in a steadfast relationship. That kind of loyal attachment, she knew, required great compromises and thoughtful consideration of another person's needs and desires above your own. Successful relationships, she knew from watching her parents, was like a lingering conversation, where the partners quietly listen and carefully considered the other's point-of-view. As equals, they didn't walk in each other's shadows, but created a new conjoined shape upon the world.

"I'm not worried about you gettin' on without me," Peter'd teased at their farewell gathering. "I'm sure Isaac's quite willin' to keep your nights and weekends fully occupied."

"Maybe," she offered in return with a sly wink. "He does have the law on his side."

"I am goin' to miss you," Peter admitted and then he kissed her. She allowed that kiss and many more before telling him that she'd miss him too.

"It won't be the same...," she began, "but it shouldn't be. What we've shared these last few weeks is that big breath of air you take in that keeps you from drowning when the dark days come. We'll always have... ."

"Paris," Peter said, quoting his favorite line from *Casablanca*. "*If not, then we got it back last night.*"

"You make a rather good Bogart," Lisbeth replied, gently touching his two-day growth with the back of her hand. She liked her men a little bit scruffy.

"*I was born when you kissed me,*" Peter replied quoting Bogart again, this time from *A Lonely Place*. "*I died when you left me. I lived a few weeks while you loved me.*"

"And so it was with me - as well," Lisbeth agreed, as tears welled in her eyes.

Their last kiss lasted until both of their breaths gave out, but their embrace continued unabated until the sun set and the city's yellow lamplights began to glow.

It was 1:17 in the afternoon when the Southwest Chief (a double story train) pulled out of the Lamy Depot. A fragrant wind full of diesel fumes and sage washed over him - clearly signaling the beginning of his eastward pilgrimage. The overnight succession of stops and stations would take Peter through the remaining three-quarters of New Mexico, into Colorado, across Kansas and Missouri, with a transfer to the Lake Shore Limited (a low bridges and tunnel friendly kind of locomotive) into Illinois. From there, he'd cross the breadth of Indiana, Ohio, the northern-western shoreline of Pennsylvania - terminating his journey in Schenectady, New York. From there it'd be easy enough to catch a Greyhound the rest of the way north to the Adirondacks.

The last few nights spent making love to Lisbeth hadn't allowed for much sleep and that lack of slumber was suddenly weighing heavily upon him - not that he would've had it any other way. Given the choice, Peter would've loved lying down in a bunk, but he couldn't afford the price of a sleeper, so he had to go back to his seat and stretch out as best he could.

From his window seat, Peter could just make out brief glimpses of hazy sagebrush as the train flew by them in the darkness. He leaned in closer. Were those series of red flashes the glowing eyes of coyotes? Wait. Were those tall waving shadows men working on the line or just Saguaro cactus? Even though he was passing through a dry and seemingly lifeless landscape, there was still much to admire. For a landscape painter like Peter, the views here were always captivating - especially in their unique use of both colour and strata.

Then, because of the train's evening travel schedule, he thought about how he'd be missing most of the state of Missouri as they rolled through it during the night. One of the advantages of going by rail was that, instead of having to watch the road from behind a steering wheel, you could actually sit back and see America. A thin smile crossed his lips as Peter considered, *perhaps of all the night time states, missing Missouri wouldn't be so terrible. There has to be plenty of good reasons why the locals often called their own state Misery.*

Despite the train's own random whistling, the crying of babies and other passenger noises, the constant rhythm of those heavy steel wheels clicking on the rails began to lull him to sleep. Like some giant iron metronome set low at sleepy waltz in 4-4 time - click clack, click clack, click clack. An hour of limpid visions passed through his brain, including vivid memories of his childhood Adirondack home and sporadic breathless images of the lovely Ms. Santoro - always calling him back to her bed. For a brief moment or two, behind his closed eyes, Peter could see Venetian painter Giorgione's half nude and half landscape, *The Sleeping Venus* - only this time with Lisbeth as the voluptuous reclining goddess.

Ah... those sultry High Renaissance Italians. Magnifico!

Eventually Peter would fall into a deep slumber. But, as he faded slowly from his own stark reality and his unconscious mind became more free, an interesting phenomenon can sometimes happen. In that split second before he encountered the dream state, Peter could've actually seen me sitting there beside him - if he'd wanted to. The moment, usually just before achieving full REM, is both fleeting and unstable. Try as I may, I've never been able to do it - going from my realm into yours. Too bad that he couldn't capture the opportunity, for it would've been grand seeing his wide-eyed expression upon recognizing me. Even as a teenager, Peter was always so very glad to see me. A fellow could survive a month in the desert with just a wee taste of that love and admiration.

When sleep did come, Peter dreamed in earnest - with the train car's ceiling becoming a panoramic projection screen. In that visual reverie he heard my voice calling out to him from the past. Behind his closed eyes Peter saw floating colours, blending and gathering into recognizable shapes and forms. A perfect world gleaned from his memory's core was unfolding before him. When the echoes of my voice faded, Peter saw himself standing on the crest of a hill bathed in golden sunlight. Below his college freshman self was the shimmering sapphire oval of a 12-acre man-made lake.

Then he heard me ask him, "see that bend in the Hudson there Peter?" The sound of my warm baritone reminded the sleeping man that even though he was no longer a child, he still missed his old mentor (and I'm very grateful for that). The once sturdy image of Gabriel Mullaney, completely enthralled about where they were and what was about to happen, came into his mind's eye. My hair and beard were dark auburn then, not all grey and drained of colour like they were when he last laid eyes on me. In animated tones and swooping gestures I continued my little speech, "that's why Mr. Church decided to put in that pond. By his aesthetic estimation, the natural view needed better symmetry."

"I remember this day," Peter mumbled in his slumber. "It was glorious!"

"Balance," I'd added silently by moving my palms up and down like a scale. "Balance for him was essential."

"You're right!" a young Peter had reasoned as he looked at the distant sparkling water. "The curve in the river perfectly balances the visual weight of the pond... ."

"Church was a scenic master!"

The landscape below us was a lush green carpet broken only by the swirling Hudson, the man-made pond, and the burnt-umber roadway that wound its way passed us and then up around the steep slope above. We were in a landscape painter's garden of Eden.

"Church had it all planned out," I'd told Peter that day. "Nothing within this 300-acre estate has real total randomness any longer, for the master altered nature everywhere to suit his own unique aesthetic."

Then I remember turning around, for something ahead in the trees had renewed my excitement. "Peter! Look!" I remember shouting. "Can you believe the grandeur of that house?"

Peter saw me silently pointing at a stone structure perched high on the hill. Even in my silence he heard me yelling, "look at the colours my boy. The colours! All the other buildings in Columbia County shall always pale in comparison to this house."

"This place is even more spectacular than Mr. Cole's house," Peter had said, still almost breathless from the view. "I've never seen such grand houses in all my life as we've seen today. They're even bigger and better than the great Camp Sagamore and that's pretty big!" Then, running with his arms outstretched, a child-like Peter gushed, "I've never been around this many open fields before. My Adirondacks is mostly made of trees."

"Church planted thousands and thousands of trees as well," I'd replied, as we started walking up the hill, "so they too, like so many brushstrokes, could be part of his overall design for this exquisite landscape."

As part of his continuing education, now that I'd successfully pulled him out of Atwell's dungeon of unenlightenment, I thought he should see some of the local sites. That day, we'd taken the opportunity to stop down at Cedar Grove, painter Thomas Cole's house in Catskill, New York on our way here. It seemed important to show young Peter multiple examples of how a career in art could be both successful and sustainable.

"It's too bad my father didn't want to join us on this trip," Peter had offered, with youthful optimism, though he really didn't miss dealing with Atwell's incessant rancor. In all truth, it was nice just spending time alone with his teacher (and I'm grateful for that too).

I'd been here myself as a much younger man, along with my father Owen and my own very silent mentor Mr. Lansing - the instigator of the devious plot to view the residence's interior. This was in the time when the artist's son Louis Church had just died and his lovely wife Sally still lived in their fine house on the hill. In 1943 the house wasn't open for public tours like it is today, so crafty Mr. Lansing, sensing how very much my father needed to be in *this* place at *this* time, surreptitiously snuck us in when dear Sally wasn't looking.

I'd met Mr. Lansing when I was but a young lad working after school in a furniture store. He was sort of the artist-in-residence there, doing both advertising and in-store promotions. The truth was, he'd caught me red-handedly stealing art supplies from his workroom, but rather than cut off my hands and convict me of theft, he chose instead to teach me all about calligraphy and compositional structure. He obviously saw artistic promise in my choice of swag.

The painting that had so captured my father's imagination was a New England landscape that perfectly depicted the brief respite that often comes after a violent storm. The painter, he would later learn was named Frederic Edwin Church and it had amazed Owen that this man could capture the very essence of what it felt like after enduring such a near calamity. The anxious rage of nature's power was suddenly gone and the blonde rays of new hope were just returning. The painting held a certain allure to the homesick Irishman. It was dated 1849 and was extremely detailed - looking almost photographic. As was the style of the time, the picture showed no signs that a brush had ever spent any time working its canvas. The finished result was as though nature had simply been filtered by a capable human hand. It was the painting's optimism and innocence that ensnared Owen's imagination. For my father, the landscape seemed to capture the rural spirit of a wild America - one that, even as it was being settled, still yearned to remain untamed and unbridled. The dense greenness of the high rolling hills bespoke of his childhood Ireland and the farmhouse that his Grandfather had built could be that tiny mill painted beside the river. The spreading clouds and the sudden reprieve from the rain all called to him from his lush Celtic memory.

"Thank you Gabe, for arranging this tour," Peter had said as he turned and looked back down the hill. "This is a dream come true for me." The excited lad was briskly shaking my hand as he continued, "ever since I first saw his painting *Landscape in the Adirondacks*, I've been intrigued by Mr. Church's work. What a picture! It so reminded me of home. Before seeing that landscape, I thought only portraits could actually speak to a person. I plan on reading everything that I can find about him."

There was a wide satisfied grin growing on my face.

"Now, thanks to you, I'm actually going to visit his home - Olana."

It was a shimmering palace hovering majestically on the crest of the hill - part Germanic Gothic castle, part Persian mansard, and part Neapolitan villa. By anyone's measure this was certainly an artist's home for it looked both serenely mystical and deftly handcrafted at the same time. The perfect physical manifestation of an unchecked artistic temperament. Unlike the log cabins, and even the Great Camp Sagamore back home in Peter's world, with their predictable wooden slabs and granite chimneys, the building before us was festooned with intricate brickwork of many colours. Rectangles swam within rectangles and diamonds danced inside of diamonds. Splendidly carved wooden borders crept boldly around each window and tower. The house's brightly coloured cornices appeared to have upside-down painted gardens on them. It was as though the geometrical floral designs imprinted there had actually blossomed and born fruit. The brightly tiled roof had a half dozen pseudo-Moorish inspired towers sprouting from it here and there like mushrooms. Neither Peter or I had ever seen a roof shingled so. In perfect serial imagery, the elegant pointed arch at the center door was also echoed in the windows and bell tower. They all were complementary elements living within a masterful design.

Standing there, some one hundred and twenty years after the house was built, it seemed to us that Church clearly foresaw that today's endless azure sky would complete the satisfying harmony of his building's vermillion and tawny façade. The forward-seeing artist had certainly planned it all well.

"I have made about one and three-quarters miles of roads this season, opening entirely new and beautiful views," Church had written to a friend in 1884. *"I can make more and better landscapes in this way than by tampering with canvas and brush in the studio."*

To their credit, Church's son Louis and his wife Sally had decided that even though their tiny family was now living in the 37-room house, they would continue to maintain and protect his father's artistic vision. Because of them and a two-year anti-development campaign led by scholar David C. Huntington, the house and property still survives as Church originally planned it today.

"Imagine a house and the lands surrounding it as a work of art," I had told Peter as we stepped up onto the stone patio. Peter paused beneath some gold Islamic lettering as I continued to explain, "a three dimensional painting is what this place is. Created by the most famous landscape painter of his time." Then as I ran my fingers along the red and yellow tiles that surrounded the archway, "There's absolutely no doubt in my mind that the design of this house was vastly influenced by the painter's travels throughout the Middle East."

"That's pretty far away," Peter had replied.

"Some 6,000 miles or more. Quite a distance in Mr. Church's time."

"We can't stay very long," Mr. Lansing had silently warned us on my first visit here. I know now why he'd pointed so anxiously at his wristwatch.

"Sally will only be gone for an hour or so," my father had added. *"It's grand that Mr. Lansing has arranged it so that we could tour the house without disturbing the family."*

For a taciturn man, Mr. Lansing was a wonderful liar.

The wide door opened onto a square vestibule, its deep purple colour reminiscent of the irises blooming in the stairway garden outside. Peeking through the house and down the long hallway, we could see a beautiful landscape framed within a pointed arch. Unable to restrain his enthusiasm, Peter pulled me through a silver stenciled doorway and into the house's east parlor.

"This is where Frederic and his wife Isabel would have had their guests wait after their long journey

getting here," I remember my father reciting, before repeating the words myself to Peter. "*See how dark and soothing this room is with the wooden shades drawn?*"

The room was certainly calming with its deeply etched antique furniture and welcoming fireplace. The door beside the hearth opened onto a small covered porch. The view through its wide pointed arch revisited the bend in the river below. To our right was the house's center court hall with more brightly stenciled arches framing each wall. There were doors leading off that main room in every direction.

"*Look Da!*" a fresh-faced Gabriel had cried out. "*Look at all those framed butterflies. They almost glow with their own light.*"

Christ! Was I ever that young?

The center room was decorated with wonderfully eclectic furniture. Painted Middle Eastern tables shared equal space with dark Rococo furniture, as well as simple Shaker rockers. The wide planked floors were mostly covered by fine multi-coloured Turkish rugs, but you could still make out their fine ochre finish beyond their fringe. It all fit together like a puzzle, a puzzle that offered real clues as to Church's many different personalities.

Before us, two full-sized brass cranes caught Peter's attention. They stood in front of an opened multi-coloured curtain, on either side of what appeared to be a narrow stage. Behind those curtains was a set of stairs leading to the second floor and a delicately carved table covered with exotic hats and scarves. My father had explained that this rather theatrical arrangement was for the putting on of plays and musicals as entertainment in a time long before radio and television. *"Guests,"* he had said, *"were encouraged to dramatically descend those very steps and recite the latest published prose - especially while wearing the appropriate hat or scarf."*

"This house is like a museum with all these treasures," whispered Peter. "But it doesn't feel like an old museum, cause everything's right out where you can touch it. You know, it almost feels like Mr. Church might return at any minute."

I recall Mr. Lansing having a rather similar expectant look upon his face, suggesting that Mistress Sally might be back at any moment and catch us in the act of breaking and entering. The scandal of being caught in such a crime motivated him greatly into hustling us along.

"Isn't that 'El Khasne, Petra', Mr. Lansing?" my father had asked, as we hurried into the Church's wide sitting room. Thrilled by how much my father knew, our anxious guide gave him an affirmative nod. *Petra* was a large painting hanging strategically above the fireplace. To me the picture looked as though a massive stone wall had violently split apart at its center, revealing a luminescent salmon coloured house. Somehow the painting brought strong feelings of safety and security to my adolescent heart. Peter saw it too. For him, the glowing coral house was also a

fortress of security positioned deep behind those dark menacing, yet protective walls.

"I read somewhere that Church selected this rose coloured marble for the fireplace specifically to complement his image of Petra," my father had added, as he inspected the nuances of the canvas. Unconsciously, his fingers were casually brushing that same luminous marble.

Mr. Lansing had pointed at two small landscapes hanging one above the other by the door. They depicted two very distinct times of day.

"Those paintings were created to celebrate the births of Frederic and Isabel's first two children," I told Peter as he unknowingly stepped over beside the ghost of Mr. Lansing. My old mentor had been following us since we'd entered the house. As was his norm, my old mentor offered no verbal commentary. Silent in life as in death I suppose. "This top one is called *Sunrise* and was painted by the master for his first born son, Herbert. The darker one below it is called *Moonrise* and it celebrates his daughter Emma. Sadly, I'm sorry to say, that both of these dear children died of diphtheria while they were both still quite young. Their deaths devastated the Churches, as it would any proud and loving parents. So, in order to get away from their familiar and now sad surroundings, Frederic and Isabel decided to take a tour of Jamaica for a time. Later, with their new son Frederic Joseph accompanying them, the Churchs spent the next two years in Europe and the Middle East. It was on that trip that Church decided to abandon the old homestead and began to truly envision his unique new home."

Clearly saddened by the thought of the Church's devastating loss of both children, I decided to take Peter outside onto the veranda so that he could get some air. A warm wind, filled with summer blossoms and early evening dew, felt good as we breathed its comforting aroma in. The piazza was long and narrow and gently patrolled on each side by a long row of finely stenciled columns.

"Perhaps their young deaths had effected a positive change for Mr. Church," Peter had said, finally breaking the silence. "Maybe Herbert's and Emma's sad deaths changed how he now looked at things. Maybe they had to die before he could envision this new and safer... castle?"

"That's certainly one way of looking at it... ."

"Picture it. There before him were his worst fears realized, the deaths of his only children. Somehow the family managed to survive such a terrible tragedy and in that mourning, he created an improved world - one that could hopefully better defend his future family."

Like Peter, back then I was still young enough to believe that everything happened for a reason. That there must be some divine plan by which all of nature's creations must follow. The idea of random choice and unrestrained chaos hadn't yet pierced either of our young and optimistic consciousnesses. For me, I had no way of knowing then that Church's dire fate would one day be my own - for the future held that there would also be the death of a beloved child for me as well.

Together, we walked over to the railing and looked down the steep hill. The majestic view of the Hudson returned in the distant west and the sparkling waters soothed our slowly evaporating trepidations.

"What a remarkable place," Peter had offered, obviously overwhelmed.

"It truly is," I had replied. "Imagine being able to create a home that actually reflects your own personality. Not some four-cornered place that you rented from some absentee landlord where every floor and apartment looks exactly the same, but uniquely yours. Imagine being bold enough and confident enough to speak to the world-at-large through all these wonderful shapes and vibrant colours."

This is what it truly means to be an artist, I have often thought to myself while contemplating Olana. *To have had a vivid and significant effect on your place in the world and to have done so primarily for your own self-satisfaction.*

"We'd better get a move on," I had said, as we stepped through a wide archway into Church's painting studio. The room's walls were brushed in an Cochineal red with a subtle gold trim. By his easel, we were able to see the very tools that had been used to create some of our most favorite works of art. Church had painted for nearly thirty years in New York City before he moved all his equipment into this new studio.

The pungent smell of linseed oil and turpentine entered Peter's nose and he found the smells wonderfully familiar. I noticed them too, as we exchanged a knowing look. It was as though Church's still brushes and dried paints were talking directly to us in the only way they could, through their enduring aroma. Peter stood where the artist must have stood, his height and weight about the same by comparison. There was Church's easel, his pallet, and all the images that he'd so often called upon for inspiration. The Mexican statuary. The suits of armor. And as always, the everlasting Hudson River flowing freely outside the window. Peter picked up a brush and rolled it gently along his open palm. Then he picked up Church's pallet and struck a pose beside the easel. The fragrant oils surrounded him and suddenly a hundred compositions flashed through his brain. It was as if the artist's tools still held countless imaginings within them, requiring only a specific talent or point of view to be released. It was a sensation that never left him.

There, behind Peter, was the framed arched landscape he had seen when we entered the house. It wasn't a painting at all, but a natural three-dimensional creation framed in wood and bathed in the warm sunshine outside.

"Every window's view," I told Peter, as I noticed him gazing through the glass, "is a Church composition. If you look out of any door or pane in this house, the view outside is a perfectly balanced landscape."

Peter was amazed. His first thought, as was mine back when I was a boy, was would I ever achieve the wherewithal to do this kind of visual magic one day myself?

"I was told that Church prepared a very special panorama outside his wife's bedroom window," I had continued. "It was arranged so precisely that his beloved Isabel was greeted by a most magnificent view each morning - without her ever having to lift her head from the previous night's pillow."

Mr. Lansing's ghost seemed preoccupied as he paced back and forth before the studio's outer door. My recollection of him was that he'd become quite agitated by a noise originating from the other side of the front door. With a flickering wave of his now translucent hand, he once again beckoned us to follow him down a hallway. Back in my youth, we had raced through the gallery hall and into Church's library, dutifully following Mr. Lansing's lead, before stopping abruptly when our leader saw something move outside the next window. With a few more violent waves of his hand, Mr. Lansing commanded us to follow him. Thankfully, one of the corner doors leading off of the court hall opened onto the servant's wing. We three errant visitors ran down those stairs and out through the back door below the kitchen. We made our way stealthily around the outside of the studio, pausing only occasionally to check and see if we were being pursued. We ended up hiding below the decking of the west verandah. When Mr. Lansing judged that the coast was clear, we dashed madly down the hill beyond the piazza, running head-long towards the river.

"You didn't get permission to go in there today did you Mr. Lansing?" my clever father had asked, already surmising the correct answer. The little man simply shrugged his tiny shoulders, and after clamping a firm hand onto his hat, ran even faster down the hill.

"Did we just break and enter that house Da?" I had asked, finally beginning to comprehend the situation. It was the only reason I could see for us running so fast.

"We entered, that's for certain lad," Da had answered, *"but as far as I can tell we didn't break anything - now did we?"*

Da and I were running as quickly as we could and still we couldn't catch up to the sprinting Mr. Lansing. Who knew that a man of his advanced age could run so rapidly?

We never did discover how my dear mentor knew that Olana would be unoccupied that afternoon. We only knew that he'd given us both a wonderful gift.

"We saw something really special today though didn't we?" I remember whispering to my father in the car on our way home.

"Aye and that we did lad," Owen had replied with a happy glint of light in his eyes, watching that magnificent edifice fade into the trees within his rearview mirror.

Today, with the presiding New York State Parks Commissioner's hearty approval, Peter and I calmly strolled the same route we'd taken in haste so long ago, taking our time to examine everything without fear of interruption - or arrest. Obviously, being a world famous artist myself then had its benefits.

Church was a member of the famed Hudson River School - an American art movement lasting some 45 years. It was heavily influenced by romanticism and exemplified by the varied talents of a diverse collection of like-minded landscape painters. While sometimes international in subject, their view of nature as a manifestation of the divine, usually depicting dynamic scenes of the Catskills, Adirondacks, and White Mountains - all of which spoke so intimately to young Peter's specific world of reference. The School's founder was Thomas Cole, Frederic Church's mentor and teacher, and also included Asher Durand, John Frederick Kennett, Jasper Cropsey, and Albert Bierstadt. Their realistic and detailed works often depicted nature as being in complete harmony with man - a fairly romantic idea considering our nation's more violent tendencies. In retrospect, this idealized dream may have been a necessary emotional reciprocal, as the horrors of our American Civil War ended only five years before The Hudson River School finally dissipated, being replaced by the softer French Barbizon style initially embraced by George Inness (the leading America artist-philosopher of his generation).

Just so you know, after Peter Atwell Phillips, Inness is my most favorite landscape painter.

PART TWO

As Peter's train was pulling into the station at Schenectady, an hour and a half north, Saoirse was near Speculator Mountain struggling to open Lorraine's old front door. Fumbling with her crutches while juggling house keys was almost more than she could handle in the dark. The cabin always had plenty of *charged-particles* (at least it did whenever Lorraine and I used to make love), but there was no evidence of electricity as she approached her new home. Unfortunately, Boyd Breedlove, our long-retained caretaker, hadn't thought to leave a light on when he reopened the place in anticipation of Saoirse's imminent arrival.

Can't really blame him though. Knowing the fellow for some years, it's my best guess that Boyd either caught a whiff of some fine smokin' tobacco, a trace of scintillating yet undefined perfume, or a gentle sniff of some well-aged whisky and followed that smell south to Lake Pleasant - incapable of stopping himself. Don't get me wrong. Mostly Boyd was a good and conscientious kind of guy, but his pernicious vices often caught'em up short. Regrettably, tonight was one of those times.

Saoirse managed to get through the screen and oak front doors before spilling the contents of her purse all over the living room floor. She'd been rummaging through her monstrous bag for a flashlight and caught a toe on the braided rug. Frustrated, she flung her crutches angrily into a corner and hopped on one foot across the still deeply shadowed room. Blindly, she moved forward. Then using the back of the couch as a viable landmark, she worked her way westward towards the nearest lamp - and switched it on.

I take full credit here for my niece's sudden and much welcomed illumination, for it was I who bought Lorraine those fine Tiffany lamps found at either end of that well-worn Van Den Berg leather couch.

Tired from her long journey up from New York City, Saoirse collapsed on the sofa and slowly looked about the room. She was glad to see that the house was still fully furnished. And why shouldn't it be? That house, stacked to the rafters, contained all of the eclectic furniture my new wife had joyfully collected over the last 50 and some-odd years. It was an antique dealers dream. Directly across from her was a peach-coloured 1930s Art Deco Waterfall cabinet that still hid our "rather gauche" television set. On either side of that was a pair of reupholstered knock-off Louis XV chairs. They were just the right kind of uncomfortable for stealthily motivating any unwanted guests to want to leave. Opposite the front door was a Merton Gershon chest that Lorraine swears she found abandoned along the highway. *"It must have fallin' off of a truck,"* she'd said while pulling the damn thing in through the front door all by her lonesome. My darlin' wife was certainly not light-fingered, but in my childhood that particular phrase always meant something that's been stolen.

When we moved into the bigger house down in Nutting, only new and comfortable furniture would do. Whenever I complained about the cost, Lorraine would remind me that it was all on my account, as nature - slowly over time - had seen fit to erase most of my once sinewy ass.

Exhaustion cured her scattered insomnia, at least for the first few nights, for sleeping in a new place always unnerved her. The random nuances of creaking floorboards, expanding hot-water pipes, and rustling trees brushing window panes took time to aurally absorb and accept as the innate music of the house. That long sought restfulness all changed as the once new moon's light began to return. First the lunar glow was nothing more than bestrewn chalk dust about the edges of the furniture and curtains. A playful phosphorescence sprinkled at the whim of a child. Then as the succeeding nights passed, its reflected light grew stronger and stronger - becoming random pastel sketches that harshly dissected the room in bold jagged arches.

When she did manage to dream, Saoirse found herself returning to visions of life in her thirties. Mostly events that were welcoming and seemed on their surface to be both serene and reassuring. But the unconscious mind is a tricky thing. Even when you least expect it, feared realities can rear their ugly heads and snap at you.

Saoirse is now forty-two years old.... a swell looking forty-two if you ask me.... but by her reasoning, nearly beyond the age of successfully bearing a child. Even though, as a man, I could father a child any time since puberty's sweet release, I fully understood her fear of that creeping time clock for motherhood. Her's, like so many others, would be a lost opportunity to give and receive unconditional love, improve the world's group dynamic, and experience a singularity of devoted purpose. Like me own mother, raising children would not only be her salvation, but a grand donation to society's overall betterment. Saoirse's best possibility to accomplish this fine female-only coup d'état was when she was married to that rat-bastard Richard. Fortunately for the world, Richard felt absolutely no need to reproduce. That single mercurial element in his DNA was the best thing about him. Only rarely since her much needed divorce had Saoirse found a man worthy enough to qualify in the pursuit of reproduction. The majority of the unsuspecting applicants were a banal collection of either self-obsessed momma's boys, litigious mouthpieces, or overaged juvenile delinquents.

Though rare, there were exceptions that both ignited her brain and tugged at her loins. One such man was Chord Lyric Murtagh, a Scotsman, who's physical topography, even fully kilted, surely thrilled every woman (and most men) that encountered him. He was tall, but not in the way one finds at all threatening. He just had to stand in the back row whenever group photos were taken. His thick auburn hair was worthy of a balding man's jealousy (and I should know). As to his intelligence, all one had to do was talk with him. His soft baritone, thoughtful demeanor, and forthright discourse were all a joy to behold. Thankfully, his absolute obliviousness of any of these fine qualities only enhanced his overall appeal.

If memory serves, me father Owen, the neighborhood Milkman, made his wee delivery of cream on my behalf when he was almost forty-five years of age. Me darlin' mother Maura accepted that tiny spit of dairy with some enthusiasm, I suspect, at just this side of thirty-four.

You'll pardon me wee brogue here, as thinkin' of me ma and pa always brings it out in me. They both had such a pleasant lilts that it makes me heart sing just thinkin' of it. Aye. Just to be called home to supper is a memory of delight, for Maura could insert love in both her food and word without effort.

There was at least one similar act performed in creating me older brother Vincent - as he was indeed conceived in the traditional manner - and as many as a baker's dozen in order to conceive me. Obviously, Maura and Owen had grown disillusioned with their first born's brashness and guile and really wanted to start their tribe over with me. If I wanted to be truthful, instead of boastful, it was more likely they were looking to have a girl. Me mother would have loved having a sympathetic confidant and solid ally against a household full of men. While Owen, the dear man once confided, had always dreamed of walking his daughter down the aisle one fine summer's day - as secretly did I, also being the father of just sons. It was not to be.

"*Women are powerful beings,*" Owen once told me by way of explaining his desire to sire a girl. "*They, unlike us, have the power to create life. If there is a supreme being in this world, it is by definition a woman.*"

As with all men since the beginning of the human race (or throughout the entirety of all the animal kingdoms for that matter) men, while necessary to the act of procreation, are more court jester than an equal king to a woman's status as queen. By my experience, it's always been our job to entertain. To amuse and occasionally inseminate... and then stay the hell out of the way.

With each pending birth, my darlin' wife Siobhán proved my father's theory, as she blossomed into a plump golden goddess - fully imbued with the power of giving life. Sadly, my dear Lorraine never had children of her own. Although, as a gifted teacher, she fully utilized her ability to kindly influence hundreds of boys and girls in the rights and practices of thoughtful kindness. In dreams for my niece, I always saw Saoirse as being a mother as well. The scope of her sheltering love should not've been squandered solely on a surly husband or some dimwitted lover, but shared with as many children as she desired.

In her dream, Saoirse was remembering a disastrous telephone call from that Scotsman Chord Murtagh. He had news that he knew she should hear only from him. It was six months since their torturous breakup, and the first time they'd spoken since that terrible day.

Also in the room that memorable evening when Chord's call came in, was Silas Madigan, Saoirse's current paramour. While he was an amiable fellow, possessing many fine qualities of his own, such as wealth and stability, he was not the *one* and she knew it. The *One* was now on the telephone telling her - as gently as he could - that he was newly engaged and about to be married to another woman.

Ever at the ready and thrilled at their few joyful months together, Silas had already suggested that he and Saoirse should marry. He was looking to settle down now that his grad-school years were over and he'd landed a decent job assisting pilots in the landing of their planes at LaGuardia - no stress there. Like most ambitious fellows, he was looking for the whole enchilada - love, marriage, a swell house, six babies in as many years, and a vacation home in Cancun. She wanted none of it... at least not with Silas Madigan.

"We could live with my folks for a while," Silas was saying, sitting anxiously on the edge of a hassock in Saoirse's front room. Her being on the telephone in the hallway hadn't slowed his thought processes down one bit. He obviously had big plans for both of them. "Just until we can get our feet under us. Shouldn't take more than six months to five years... ."

"I've got a steady income," Saoirse yelled back, cupping her hand over the mouth piece. "There's no need for anyone to stay with your parents." Then directing her thoughts to Chord, she asked plaintively into the phone, "how long of an engagement? This all seems to be happening way too fast."

"Nae too long," Chord answered, not seeing how being more accurate about the date would be any easier on her. "It's most only an idea reit noo. naethin' etched in stone... ."

"Or embossed stationary," Saoirse hopefully whispered.

"Yeah... I get that," Silas agreed regarding their staying at his parent's house. "I just want to hold up my share. Training at the airport might take months and I won't get my full salary until I'm fully certified."

"Who is this woman?" Saoirse asked, afraid that this mystery woman was part of his reason for having broken up with her.

"A woman Ah mit in college," Chord replied. "Ye don't know 'er."

"You're moving way too fast," Saoirse said loudly enough so that both men could hear her.

"The heart wants what the heart wants," Silas replied warmly, not seeing any reason for them to wait.

"It's whit she wants," Chord admitted. "She asked me. I'm in, but Ah need mair time... ."

"To forget me?"

"No. Saoirse," Chord replied truthfully, "Ah coods ne'er do that."

"Then why… ."

"Aren't we together… ?"

"Yeah. That!"

"We awreddy gone thru aw this… ."

"But how could you get married so soon after rejecting me?"

"Ah ne'er rejected ye. Ah jist wasn't sure that Ah lov'd ye enoogh… ."

"Enough to… ?"

"Have children."

"Maybe we could just live here," Silas continued, still following his original train of thought. "The airport's not such a bad commute from Queens."

"That's not negotiable," Saoirse replied to Chord, feeling all of the heat return from her original conversation with him on the matter of raising a family. Everything had been going so well, even beyond happy, until she posed that particular question.

"Not negotiable? You don't want to live here after we're married?" Silas was at a loss. Her apartment was far superior to his. "I get that it's a six-floor walkup, but we're both young… ."

"Yeah. Ah know that's nae negotiable," Chord answered wearily. "That's wa I'm here with her an' yoo're thaur with heem."

Saoirse looked over at Silas. There he was earnestly trying to reason how they could survive as a couple, all while she was there hanging by a thread for the love of another man. There was a lot about Silas that was attractive. He just wasn't Chord Murtagh.

"Ah only called tae lit ye know," Chord explained, returning to the reason for contacting her so out-of-the-blue. "Ah dinna want ye tae hear it from one of uir mutual friends."

"OK."

"OK? … we'll live here?" Silas wanted to know.

"OK. Thanks for telling me," Saoirse replied, drained of emotion. "I hope you both will be very happy."

From where Silas was sitting, he could barely make out Saoirse's expression, as only a single candle burning in the kitchen cast any light on her face. It looked like she was crying, but he couldn't tell for sure. Nothing he'd said should have made her tear-up - unless they were tears of joy.

After she hung up the telephone, allowing Chord to disappear forever into the ether, Saoirse slowly walked back into the front room. She knew what had to be done. Her feelings for the Scotsman were still too real to be ignored and in all good conscience, she couldn't leave Silas just hanging. He deserved so much better.

"I'm sorry."

"Sorry for what?"

"Having to say goodbye… ."

"What? I'm leaving? Silas answered, confused. "I've only just got here. We haven't even ordered the pizza yet."

"It's not working."

"The phone?" he was still confused as to her meaning. That's who he thought she'd been on the phone with all this time. "No problem. We can use my cell to order a pie."

"No. Silas. *We're* not working."

"But... ?" Her expression stopped him cold. There was little doubt that she had affection for him. Silas could see it in all the little everyday ways, but Saoirse didn't *love* him. Not in the way he wanted or deserved.

"I thought I was free," she began, her eyes continuing to tear up. "But I'm not. Not in any way that matters."

"I can wait... ," he offered hopefully, "until whatever's binding you fades away."

"For eternity?" she replied with absolute sincerity. "Because that's how long it might be before I'm free to love again."

This sullen event was not a complete surprise to him. There'd always been a reluctance on Saoirse's part to completely let her guard down with him - as though something still held her strings. He had earnestly hoped that his unique collections of wit and charms might have eventually wore her down - breaking her emotional chains.

"How about, we order that pizza anyway," Silas offered hoping to throw her a lifeline, "and we don't think any more about it?"

He hated having to play the friend card, but she did seem so pitifully unhappy. Leaving her alone in such despair seemed unwise - especially when he loved her so. At least this way, she might remain in his life a little longer - maybe even long enough to cure her of her pain.

"Just so long as you know it's over between us." Saoirse replied, glad at retaining a friend and not having to be alone just now.

"OK. I can accept that," Silas offered with a grin, "But you can't eat up all of the slices of pepperoni like you always do."

"Deal," she replied, looking gratefully up at him. Her expression didn't give him false hope, just the knowledge that he'd done the right thing.

Now, I've known a lot of different kinds of men in my lifetime. Good men. Sad men. Hilarious and hateful men. Men who didn't deserve the air they were breathing and men who very much *did,* and spent far too little time on this earth breathing than I. But, if any one of them told me, in all honesty, that they didn't want to have a child, I'd have to believe them. I'd have to accept their bold pronouncement as fact. After all, it's not something you easily deny yourself. For once taken, it's a road that can't be easily retraced or possibly ever found again. Among other things, a man, caught in arriving at that decision might have to admit that he hasn't enough fortitude to be a father - good or bad.

He might say, *"this world that we live in isn't a fit place to raise a child, and I've neither the stamina nor understanding to fix it."* In my way of thinking, a man can only successfully transform the tiny orb that he's intimately enmeshed in. The wider world is far too grandiose and political, and therefore beyond any one individual's ability to control. Fix what you can fix, and live with that.

Or he might tell himself, *"I can't afford the hundreds of thousands of dollars that it'll take to raise a child to adulthood."* As if anyone could ever save enough money before taking such a leap. *"But then again, a child might stand in my way, preventing me from becoming the world's next billionaire."* Obviously, such a selfish man shouldn't have children, for he must feel that there aren't enough hours in the day to be both moneymaker and doting father.

"There needs to be a stability of family before such a monumental thing should be attempted," another man might reason. As if any family could be so perfectly balanced. Families - by any definition - are most often a collection of crazy people simply bound together by either blood or marriage. *"You only get to pick your friends,"* my grandsons used to tell me.

"There are too many diseases on this planet. Too many chances at deformity." As though life offers any such protective guarantees. My dear Michael was born perfect - absolutely perfect. He boasted ten fingers and ten toes and yet, time and evil circumstance colluded, first robbing him of nearly 80% of his sweet body and then 100% of his life - all well before his time. Would I still have gone down that road? Not had that dear boy, if I knew how it would all finally turnout in the end? I'll answer only for myself.

Yes!

Yes, I would. If only to have experienced the hope we shared during Siobhán's troubled pregnancy. The moment of his birth. His first steps. The potty training with M&Ms. Teaching him to read. Being there when first he heard Jack Bruce sing. Showing him my art, and awakening creativity in him - if even for only such a truncated span of time. Being the man I am (was), even without having actually experiencing them, the loss of those precious moments would be (have been) devastating to me.

So, when Chord Murtagh flatly refused to have children with my dear Saoirse, I have to take him at his word. Was he afraid to bring children into this shit-hole of a world? Maybe. Was he concerned that he couldn't provide a good home or ample nourishment or did he just NOT like children? That I couldn't say - at least for right now. All that is true, is that Murtagh felt a doubt. Whether that nagging uncertainty was sincerely felt or a simple convenience against being tied-down, it should still hold great sway over any decision to not procreate. Until that cognitive hesitation is dissolved by either reason or love, it should be well heeded. An unwanted child bears a terrible burden in this world.

An example of which, is Saoirse's ex-husband who currently resides in a maximum security state prison for aggravated murder - of a child. It's a hard place for a life-long cop, but a just place for his thoughtless crime. Richard Delaney should have stuck to his plan of never having children, even if they weren't his biologically, and he'd most likely still be a free man right now. Although, even as a sworn devotee of the city's grand *protect and serve* policy, he wasn't very good at either. One procedural shortcut or another would have likely landed him in jail anyway. Bribes, looking the other way, and brutality of minorities had always been his skewed way of sheltering and providing succor to the public. He was a criminal in blue.

It may have simply been inexperience, overwhelming frustration, or an absolute hatred of another man's sperm. I'm guessing all three. Like many a baby killer before him, Richard had little regard for anything concerning the child's father. Mentally, the man's innocent offspring was always a stark reminder that someone had made love to Delaney's new girlfriend before he had. The incessant crying. The sleepless nights. The love and attention offered by his paramour to another human being instead of him, all played against the child's survival. I'm not even certain that if the child had been his and Saoirse's whether the poor darlin' would've survived in his malevolent care.

It's probable that even though Delaney was given twenty years, it's most likely a life sentence. Between his being a cop and having put many of his cell-mates into that very prison, plus his having snuffed-out such an innocent life, his new world is just about as accepting as the one he'd crafted for that other man's newborn baby.

Instead of stepping outside the bedroom, and letting the poor darlin' cry it out a while on her own, Richard, ever the bully, clasped his calloused palm over the child's mouth intending to still her crying - with force - as was his norm. Of course it had the total opposite effect. Terror filled the child's excited eyes as air became harder and harder to come by. Maybe he recognized a tiny spark of femininity in her pleas to remain breathing and found it needed to be extinguished - as he'd tried so often to do with Saoirse. Or, perhaps he was just an asshole, with little or no concern for anyone else's well-being. That's my take on Delaney. A worthless man, who'll rightfully spend the rest of his pitiless existence in a dark and unforgiving place. A perfect end, given the dark abyss he so thoughtlessly sent that innocent baby girl to.

Now, back in upstate New York, as he walked about the burned-out shell of the old family mercantile, Peter considered his father Atwell again, this time from a more distant perspective - as that of a young boy. Back then, like any other expectant child, all he'd ever wanted was a little affection and maybe some degree of tenderness. Real love would've been asking far too much of his old man. What Peter got instead was a suffocating cloak of near insufferable indifference. He would've enjoyed the encouraging touch of his father's hand on his shoulder - guiding him to greatness - but that was no longer in Atwell's abilities - not that they ever really were. After his wife Jenni died trying to give birth to their twin daughters, whatever goodness in him dried up. Peter knew that there had to be something of value deep in his father's character, or his dear mother would never have aligned herself so closely with him. How could such a kind woman find and enjoy intimacy with such a cold and distant bastard? If Jenni had been able to detect even a hint of devotion, passion, or sweet ardor in her husband, it had to be minute or tenuously hinged, for no signs of goodwill or altruism were able to survive her untimely passing.

"How do I grieve this man?" Peter wondered out loud to the cold charcoal timbers that surrounded him like some ersatz picket fence. In memory, Peter could once again feel the stinging of his father's belt across his bare buttocks and later the full flat of his disapproving hand across his face.

In the rubble at his feet, Peter kicked over a burnt board and found his father's old coffee cup. It'd been a gift from Jenni to her husband on their thirteenth wedding anniversary. It was brown fired clay with an owl deeply etched into one side. The inscription read: *Hoo Loves You?* Despite all the destruction around it, the cup hadn't a crack in it.

"Where were the caring embraces," he wanted to know, having seen those freely doting families flaunting their kindnesses at school functions and community picnics. Those also-flawed parents were somehow still capable of openly showing their adoration and devotion - why couldn't Atwell?

No student art show. No vibrant Springtime musicale. No gridline sporting event could compel Atwell to leave his sorry business and see his son's bourgeoning accomplishments. For some unexplained reason the old man saw no point in attending. Peter'd never be a famous artist, nor some variety singer or dancer on TV, and certainly not a highly valued sports hero cheered on by thousands. In Atwell's limited vision, his untalented son should simply resign himself, like he did, to working in the Mercantile until his dying day.

"How do I grieve this nothingness?" he thought, looking hard at the soot covered cup. It was as empty as his father's chilled heart.

It occurred to Peter that his dry eyes now were the result of having cried himself out as a child. There was nothing left. No reservoir of tears for cruel Atwell now that he was dead.

The neighbor's letter that found him in Santa Fe reported that Peter's father had been thoroughly waked and satisfactorily buried. Though he hadn't bothered to mention where the grave site was. Peter only cared about the grave's location so that he wouldn't stumble over it by accident some day. He had absolutely no intention of ever intentionally visiting the spot. Being here at the Mercantile was horror enough. The only certainty was that Atwell's final resting place couldn't be side-by-side with Jenni's, as she and his tiny lost sisters' ashes were no doubt re-burned in the recent mercantile fire. Absently, Atwell had set their shared urn in a cluttered storeroom, meaning to find a more proper place for their exhibition and simply forgotten them.

"This burned out legacy is what you deserve old man!" Peter called out to the charred beams and twisted metal surrounding him. It was as if Atwell's total disdain of his fellow man had grown to such a fevered pitch that it finally ignited the dry tinder and scattered debris of his previously unchanging, yet totally decrepit store.

"You gave me nothing!" he shouted, "and yet you demanded my complete allegiance - as if we were truly co-conspirators against the world." Then softening, remembering Jenni's kindness he added, "momma loved the world and I do too, in spite of you!"

With that, he hurled his father's coffee cup hard against the stone chimney - shattering it. That charred but enduring hearth was the only source of warmth that Peter could count on in that house after his mother's death. The irony was, that it was left to Peter to rekindle the fire there every morning and maintain it throughout the day. His father couldn't be bothered. Cold was his natural state of being.

The insatiable hollowness of this deadly place was beginning to gnaw at Peter, burrowing ever so relentlessly into his very psyche. Without a second thought, he decided to walk away - intending never to return.

"This soul-sucking rubble," Peter muttered softly, as he took a half-dozen long strides out of the shadows towards the filtered sun, "would consume me whole if I mistakenly chose to remain - just like it did with my old man."

It makes me feel good that Peter visits my grave from time to time. He talks openly to me there, providing much of the information that I now set before you. Although, it fractured my already broken heart to hear Peter cry out to me that day, as he walked alone among the ashes, "Hey! Where are you ol'man?! Where be ya now that I needed ya?!"

Along with contemplating Atwell's heinous treason that day he returned to the mountains, he also recalled warm memories of me. Specifically, our first meeting - when as a teenager, he brought firewood up to my newly rented cabin. We hit it off immediately, for Peter's always been such a bright and curious boy - full of energy and wanting to know everything. Over those many months, he and I had grand chats, discussing the world and over time his possible place within it. Until we chatted, he had no real picture of himself stepping out beyond his mountain home. I like to think that it was my influence alone that set him free, but I believe his mother had much to do with it. For those first few years, when he was her only child, Jenni told him tall tales of her home across the Atlantic Ocean and beyond the River Forth. But just as often, the pain of his father's hurtful indifference would choke him quiet and it would take all my patience and sheer candor to release his staggering rigidity.

Even back then, Peter knew that whenever he considered his time spent with Atwell, it would take time to polish off the raw edges of hatred and recognize that his father was probably deeply hurting too by the loss of both his wife and his new born twins - little Marjorie and Dorothy. After all, I'm sure that even Atwell recognized that these few individuals were the only folks on the planet that might actually have cared a hoot-in-hell about him.

"It may sound wrong," Peter sadly considered, standing there at the far edge of smoky rubble, "but maybe, just maybe, it was for the best that my sisters didn't survive without a mother. Their sorry little lives would've surely been hell - just like mine - having only damnable Atwell to provide them with love and solace."

In my heart, I know that Peter didn't mean that the girls were better off being dead. Even a punished child is better off than one that's forever lost, as reclamation and reconciliation are always possible - as proven by my lad Peter's triumph over his father's biting insouciance.

Peter also understood that his old man may not have been capable of accessing his own true feelings in the matter of these sudden deaths. Atwell had never gotten any real affection from his own father, and so he'd no such historic reserves on which to rely upon. In this way, Peter kindly recognized, that both he and Atwell had equally suffered.

That being said, Peter also knew that there was always a deeply etched flaw in Atwell Phillips. A clawing desire to be off and alone, always away from his fellow man. He'd have been a hermit if not for dear Jenni's love. Without his wife, Peter had ceased to be his father's son, and had, bereft of all affection, been sorely and irrevocably jettisoned. Left on his own, Peter could only join the rest of the troubled throng in a world made up by his father's own accounting of cheats, and liars, and kings.

PART THREE

As often happens with us artist types -
especially upon our sudden demise - the world
sometimes sits up and suddenly takes notice of our
previously neglected work. With this new more hyper
interest, our rampant anonymity dries up and would-
be scholars, dubious art critics, along with a
smattering of hard-hearted charlatans step up to
examine and/or exploit our most earnest efforts -
proclaiming them masterpieces. Because of this
strange cultural phenomena, upon my death, all of my
paintings were either borrowed or bought outright by
the very prestigious Metropolitan Museum of Modern
Art in New York City. My guess is that buoyed by the
rising clarion clamor for my newly declared
masterworks and fearing that other museums might
beat them to the punch, this venerable institution
made a grand decision to acquire as many of my
modest efforts as they could. Thankfully, their sudden
ardor provided my dear wife with a more than adequate

income, but left the walls in our new Nutting house completely barren. This was bittersweet for my dear Lorraine, of course, for seeing my recent works (mostly portraits of her) hanging throughout our home had made her feel both sad and appreciated. Sad at having her companion and lover so irrevocably torn away, and appreciated for her long life and continued beauty - at least in one man's adoring eyes. So, when she came across those four threadbare paintings by unknown artists at a nearby estate auction, she bought them without a second thought. For her, the pieces not only represented a craft that I'd heartily worked with much vigor throughout my entire life, but also offered keen support and nurture, just as we'd done for Peter as he slowly gained professional momentum, to these new and no doubt struggling artists.

The first painting was of a woman in her early twenties who was looking directly out at the viewer - her deep auburn hair blending seamlessly into the dark trunk of a wide and shapely tree. A bright horizontal line dissected the image just above center - extending in a solid shape to the bottom, leaving the top third in shadow and scattered with brightly coloured leaves. It wasn't realism, but a stylized portrait, much like something I would've painted had my creative eye chanced to envision it. The artists name was Raphael Jon Dominic. The similarity of our styles is what first drew Lorraine's eye. She'd thought that it might have been one of my many lost canvases.

The second work, by Michael Bruno, was a thought-provoking oil over a yellowed newspaper collage. Painted freely on masonite board, with inspiration, no doubt, from Belgian surrealist René Magritte. Its multiple figures moved freely throughout the composition as if they were random strangers passing on a city street. Only the central figure seemed to be communicating directly with the viewer - his details remaining vague, like someone you've yet to meet.

The third painting was an impressionist inspired portrait - again of a twenty-something woman. This time artist Paul Henry allowed his model to glance slightly away, leaving her forever lost in thought. The brush strokes were thick and full of both gravitas and grace. The lone figure, sharing both colour and tone with the background, almost disappears into the stacked wooden columns on which she is gently leaning.

The final canvas, also impressionistic, documented two African men from above as they stood in the snow below the roof of a grand mausoleum. Their plaintive looks suggested a stark dichotomy of spirt. One man looks as though he has lost a kind and benevolent master, while the other appears glad at finally having attained his long-sought freedom in the overlord's timely death. The name Jefferson Mills Wait was inscribed with fervor in the lower right-hand corner, as if it'd been scratched there with the hard pointed-end of his brush.

Impressionism (a philosophy I heartily embraced), is a style of painting that originated in

France around 1860, and is characterized by its desire to depict the visual impression of a particular moment in time, through the use of shifting light and color - not to simply record the place or event as realistically as possible. Thanks to the Impressionists, emotion was now a colour within the spectrum of any artist's palette.

Immediately, Lorraine was drawn to learning more about these four men, as none of their names were the least bit familiar to her - and she, being ever curious, certainly knew her way around the world of Art. That was the way with art - or any of the arts really. People toiled earnestly at painting, music, or writing, and were either noticed - as was my kind circumstance - or sorrily neglected, as perhaps was the case with these four talented yet rather anonymous individuals. Beyond celebrity, all four of the works that Lorraine had purchased that day had real artistic value - at least to her informed aesthetic. For her, the fact that she was touched by something within each of their compositions gave the works true credence. An artistic credibility that couldn't be diminished, even if some harsh critic's voice should be in stark disagreement. The critic, Lorraine understood correctly, came from his own sphere of influence, and she from her's. While each of their individual experiences held weight - Lorraine's was greater, grown by her own years of enlightenment, while the critic's held less sway being powered solely through concurrence of strangers -

most of whom she and he would never intimately know.

"I need to share these gems with Saoirse," Lorraine thought, considering her niece's successful expertise as a biographer. "She'll know how to find out who and where and what it is about these men."

With Saoirse's input, Lorraine might just be able to fulfill one of my final mandates - the support and nurturing of new and struggling artists. It pleases me no end, that if any of these painters needed her help, she would do so in honor of me.

Certainly, Lorraine could have easily Googled each of these men on her own, but that would have prevented her from having a prime opportunity to engage with her niece. Saoirse had seemed so sad when she arrived in Nutting, before heading north to the old homestead, that it seemed like a bit of a distraction might be in order. Besides, my dear Lorraine would enjoy the hunt for information even better with an inspired partner.

This was a good thing in another way, for despite her previous assertions, Saoirse actually had no new subject for the book she was supposedly writing. After completing her substantive tome on artist William Merritt Chase, nothing of equal value or interest had jumped out to her. Her publisher had ideas, but none of them came from a place that Saoirse could claim. That lack of clarity of purpose was certainly understandable, seeing as we all now know, the girl was basically hiding in the mountains from the pain of losing her long term paramour - Chord Murtagh. The cad!

With the Mercantile in ashes all around his feet and his childhood homestead also gone up in smoke, Peter no longer had a place to stay. His first thought was checking into a motel somewhere along Route 8, but the Cedarhurst Motor Lodge at the junction of Route 30 had no vacancies for the night. On second thought, maybe Shaheen's Motel in Tupper Lake, but that was fully booked as well. His next idea was maybe checking the availability of staying at Lorraine's old house. With her now living in Nutting, he wouldn't be disturbing anyone - or so he incorrectly assumed, for he had no way of knowing that Saoirse now owned the property. Like a thoughtless child, he hadn't even bothered to tell Lorraine that he was back on the East Coast again. That was something he planned to do only if he chose to stay in New York State for a while.

The Moose Lake house was just as he remembered it - one unremarkable story of weathered smoked-grey siding, under a low dark shingled hipped-roof. As he looked beyond the untrimmed shrubbery and through the wide screened-in porch, it surprised him to see that the two front room windows were glowing with a soft amber light. Peter had only expected to find the dark loneness that is inevitable when such a property has been abandoned. After all, he knew that it was I who made Lorraine move out of her comfortable and unassuming home and into a down-state Victorian palace.

"What to do?" he thought to himself. Obviously, someone was at home or soon would be. If it were Lorraine, then all would be fine. Well beyond my many fatherly intrusions into his life, she'd been like a true second mother to the lad. But, in such a dark wood, a stranger might think him a noxious intruder - which is exactly what he would be to anyone of clear mind at this time of night. As he turned around to leave, another car pulled slowly up the driveway, effectively blocking his escape.

"Can I help you?" a woman's confident voice called out to him through an open car window.

"I was looking for Lorraine," Peter fibbed a little. He thought it best all around if he offered the stranger some kind of valid reference. He'd hate for anyone to mistake him for a Jehovah's Witness.

"Oh...I'm sorry, but Lorraine doesn't live her any more. I do."

"It's been a while between visits... ."

"Were you one of her students?"

"Yes," Peter partly fibbed again. While Lorraine hadn't actually taught him how to play the piano, she did school him on what to expect from a good strong independent woman. Through her no-holds-barred style of motherly love, Peter knew firsthand that a grand source of warmth and gentle guidance existed in the world - even for him. "I'll have to admit that I'm just a local boy returning home after a very long absence."

As Peter slowly approached the woman's car, she began the arduous process of getting herself out and up onto her crutches. Sadly, Saoirse's bum-knee still needed some support.

This time it was Peter's turn to ask, "can I help you?"

"No. I've got plenty of practice with these things," she answered. Then looking slowly over her guest and quickly evaluating him as a limited threat to her safety, she added brightly, "you could grab that grocery bag off of the front seat, if it wouldn't be too much trouble... ."

As Saoirse stepped back out of the way, Peter dutifully leaned into the car and seized the bag as requested. It was full of bread, and milk, and eggs - and three bottles of merlot. Even though their arms only brushed against each other for the briefest of moments, Peter still felt a wee spark.

Walking a few paces behind her as they both headed towards the house, Peter - even in shadow and despite the crutches - enjoyed the stunning view of the woman's shifting hips. Her short-shorts were cut that perfectly. Now, don't disparage him for looking. Peter is a trained artist after all. Taught by me-self to observe and honor beauty where and whenever it is found.

Hopping now on one foot, Saoirse pushed open the front door - without having to unlock it. Since moving here from Queens, she'd not once bothered to bolt the front door. Freedom from rampant paranoia was one of the many perks about living in the Adirondacks. Besides, if someone really wanted to get into your house, there were always plenty of chainsaws lingering about to make that happen with little fuss.

"Just put the bag on the kitchen counter, if you don't mind."

As Peter walked around her and into the kitchen, Saoirse turned on the living room light. The vintage incandescent bulb strained at delivering even three-quarters of its advertised 75 watts.

In that soft glow, Peter saw her face for the first time.

"How could it be?! he thought, with a pang of excitement. "Saoirse here?! Back in my woods after so many years?!"

His mind flew gladly back to that wintery afternoon when he drove her up to my rented cabin in a horse-drawn sleigh. The trip up from the Mercantile had been too woefully short, as far as Peter was concerned. Being side-by-side with such a lovely woman had been an unexpected treat, and having been in control of a horse and sleigh had allowed him to show off his manly skills a little. He was sure that she could see how confident he was behind the reins. They had not talked very much, but the sound of her sweet voice was like a summer wind, all warm and soothing. She had even allowed him to touch her arm as he'd helped her up into the sleigh. It was like throwing a feather pillow on a bed the way she floated up onto the seat. Women of any kind were rare in his secluded world of Adirondack hunters and woodsmen, and here was a real "looker" as Atwell used to say whenever a female was around. Peter had always felt certain that he would like women if he ever had a chance to be with one. That day had been a real good start.

Then, as he looked over at the lovely forty-something woman in the next room, Peter remembered the exact moment when he first fell in love with Saoirse. He'd offered her his hand so that she could safely descend from the carriage, and she'd gratefully accepted it. Never in all his sixteen years had he ever seen such a worldly beauty and here she was gladly accepting his course and calloused hand. Saoirse wasn't distant like those few other women he'd come across, who were mostly rich tourists or the stuck-up executive wives of the paper mill owners. Saoirse was different in important ways. She had always looked directly into his eyes when she spoke - allowing the intensity of her soul to come through. It wasn't her fault that back then he couldn't quite hold or return her ebullient gaze. Thankfully now, with years of hands-on experience under his belt, that would no longer be an issue.

"Hello Saoirse," Peter ventured softly, still marveling at her enduring winsomeness. "I don't suppose you recognize me."

His knowing her name certainly took her by surprise, rattling her some I suspect. Then looking hard at him, turning her head this way and that, hoping a distant recollection might reignite and match that roguishly handsome face with an appropriate name from their shared past. At first she drew a blank. Childhood friend? Business associate? Then slowly, as one drowsy synapse followed another, a crystalline memory of his twinkling ardent eyes sparked anew. That subtle glow of insight was followed by a quick succession of other pertinent remembrances. A frigid winter's day. A jaunty sleigh ride. An enchanting boy. When she added in tonight's details - his fine stubbled jawline, audaciously curly hair, with that soft melodic baritone - it all came to full realization.

I wish that I had a newly primed canvas and a fresh stick of charcoal so that I could've captured the look on her face when Saoirse finally recognized that it was young Peter Phillips standing there in her kitchen.

"Peter?"

"Aye Ms. Delaney. It's been a long time... ."

"I'm a Mullaney again," Saoirse admitted happily, correcting him. "I've been free of that nightmare for quite some time now."

"I can't begin to tell you how great it is to see you," Peter offered, showing much more of his inner feelings than he'd intended to. Suddenly, with a spot of anger at her ex-husband, he recalled the violet bruises on her face that day, which he'd at first thought were simply the effects of wind-burn from having ridden in the open sleigh.

"You were looking for Lorraine?" she offered, giving him an out. Saoirse could see by his fervid expression that his youthful feelings for her hadn't diminished one iota during their long separation.

"No. Not really," he admitted. "I was surprised to see that the lights were on, and only said that because I thought you'd be a stranger."

"Then, what brought you here?" she asked, partly wondering if he'd come searching for her.

"I was up looking at the old Mercantile, and found it burned to the ground." he replied, choosing to say nothing about Atwell being dead. It was best that that subject never came up, as he still wasn't sure how he felt about it all.

"How terrible... ," Saoirse replied, feeling bad that his childhood home should be so effectively erased. Then as she comprehended his sudden housing predicament, she asked, "and you were looking here for a possible place to stay?"

"Yes," Peter admitted sheepishly. "I knew that Lorraine and Gabe had moved south to Nutting some years ago and figured the place might be empty."

"It was empty, until early last month," Saoirse replied, before swinging her arms out wide like a circus barker and adding wistfully, "now it's all mine."

"Weren't you living in New York?" He'd always been so in awe of her living in such a big city. Even to this day, after traveling all across the country, he wasn't sure that he could do it.

"In Queens, actually. But that's all behind me now. At least until my knee heals."

At the mention of her knee, Peter's gaze reluctantly moved downward and away from her beguiling face.

"Bicycling accident," she answered, correctly anticipating his next question. "I should be off these crutches very soon."

"Sorry for your pain," Peter offered sincerely, captured now by her shapely bronze legs - who's tenor was the perfect balance of sinew and grace. His having lingered there so long did not escape her appreciation.

"So… You were looking for a place to stay for the night?"

"Yes, I'm afraid."

"Why not stay here?" The offer seemed to come with all available options.

"I'd hate to put you out," he lied. Being with her again, all alone in the mountains, was far beyond his most outrageous imaginings. The latent sixteen-year-old Peter was jumping for joy.

"Not at all," she replied, glad at an end to her self-exiled loneliness - if even for one night. "There's a second bedroom, with an old Murphy bed that should do you nicely."

"It wouldn't be my first wall-bed night. My college years were full of 'em."

"I was going to have some *wine*. Could I offer you some *wine*?"

"Did you mention *wine*?" They both seemed to be enjoying the sound of the word.

"Yes. Could I offer you a glass?"

"Sure. That'd be great. But why don't you let me get it and you stay off of that knee for a while?"

With a wave of her hand she gently dismissed him once again to the kitchen. "There are glasses in the high cupboard above the stove."

"I remember Miss Lorraine having them there too," Peter replied. "Not that we ever shared a glass of *wine* together."

"While you're up and about," she wondered politely, "could you please switch on the reel-to-reel and give us a bit of mood music?"

Dutiful Peter did as he was told and before handing her the glass of wine and sitting gratefully down beside her, he switched on the music - thankful that the vintage reel-to-reel would mean an hour or two of uninterrupted melodies.

As the dulcet tones of Van Morrison's *Moondance* quickly filled the room, Peter refreshed Saoirse's glass. She had drained the first one almost immediately.

"Tough day?" he asked, wondering why she'd downed the drink so quickly.

"No. Just a lonely one."

Try as he may, Peter couldn't fathom how such a beguiling woman could ever find herself being lonely. Perhaps it was because most men found her too intimidating and were reluctant to even approach her - much less make a claim on her time. He completely understood that way of thinking, for that was him - then, but Peter had true confidence - now.

After they had exhausted all of the *where have you been* and *what have you been doing with yourself* questions - plus most of that first bottle of merlot, Peter ventured into the land of the truth.

What could possibly happen when previously restrained and roisterous ardor meets a splintered psyche bathed in drunken loneliness?

"*A fantabulous night to make romance,*" Van Morrison suggested enthusiastically.

"Can I admit to you that you were and still are my first love?" The look on Peter's face was proof enough that what he'd admitted to her was true.

"I believe you just did," Saoirse whispered, glad to hear him finally say it. She'd always known about his teenage-infused puppy love, so his continuing adult fervor was a thrilling surprise. The mere idea of his having kept that initial affection so completely intact made her self-esteem blossom ten-fold.

"In all my imaginings," Peter continued to confess, "I never dreamt that one night you and I might find ourselves completely alone together."

"It's good to have dreams," Saoirse agreed, as she slowly refilled her glass. "Otherwise they can never come true."

"Did you ever have such dreams about me?" Peter wanted to ask, but he wasn't sure that his heart wanted to know the answer.

"Could you please open that second bottle?" Saoirse pleaded. "There seems to be a hole in my glass. The damn thing won't stay full."

"*And I'm trying to please to the calling,*" Van continued to croon, "*of your heart-strings that play soft and low.*"

Dutiful Peter did as she requested, but when he returned to the couch again, he dropped down right beside her. The heat of her splendid thigh against his warmed him to his toes.

"I've never known such loneliness," Saoirse began, suddenly looking wistful. Knowing that his lingering affection had been languishing for so long, suddenly emboldened her own sense of isolation.

"Here in the mountains? I can believe that. Hell. I've lived that."

"No. Peter. In New York City," she replied, throwing her head back and reveling her long shapely neck - which he immediately longed to nuzzle. Damn! He simply couldn't take his eyes off of her.

"Lonely? With those thousands of people all around you?"

"Yes. Their indifference makes it all worse. Here, you might encounter a half dozen people in a week's time and most of them will offer you a word. Kind or not, but a word. In the City, I've gone months without so much as a hello or even a go-fuck-yourself. People just don't seem to see you. I often feel quite invisible there."

"I see you."

"I see that you do and I like the way that you admire me."

"You don't mind?"

"Never. Not once since the first day we met."

"Was I that transparent?"

"Heartfelt love always is," she replied, and then by way of sincere punctuation - she leaned in and kissed him.

Like any red-blooded-American-boy, Peter repaid that singular kiss with one of his own.

Saoirse drained her glass, and then stood up. She swayed there for a moment or two trying to regain her balance. Peter, knowing exactly what to do, stood up and took her into his arms - literally sweeping her off her feet.

"Where would you like me to set you down?"

"On your Murphy bed, if it isn't too much trouble."

Saoirse and Peter meandered down the hallway together intent on trying out the springs of that old Murphy bed. Being a rather shy storyteller in this particular instance (as I know both parties really really well), I had to completely advert my eyes, so an accurate play-by-play description of what took place in Peter's bedroom will not be provided here. But, if I allow my mind's eye to roam freely about, and study on recreating the event as a painter might, it may have gone something like this:

The moon was in full glow, covering everything with a velvety patina of celestial silt, effectively bathing Saoirse's enticing angular visage in a captivating etherial light. As she slowly undressed, Peter was entranced, unable to move at first - as Saoirse's gossamer skin, pale as always, shone iridescently. Eagerly, she beckoned him to join her on the bed and he could not disobey. Lying there beside her seemed both natural and extraordinary. She was a lithe and mystical creature to his mind. Something quite fanciful and unique that'd once appeared to him long ago, completely mesmerizing his youthful psyche and then disappearing just as quickly back into the dark woods of the big city. Saoirse understood his hesitation so she took his hand and guided it down. His fingers were like shadows moving slowly along her thigh, then over her hip to that flat spot at the base of her spine. He lingered there until she beckoned him further. The moon followed his tender touch as his fingertips ventured slowly upward moving evocatively along her torso. She pulled him closer, and kissed him. Again, having Saoirse's lips upon his fulfilled a decade's old dream - and despite all his enhanced imaginings was NOT in any way a disappointment. It was a revelation! He'd rightly anticipated the warmth and duration, but the taste was almost overwhelming in its vibrancy. Saoirse rolled Peter over and straddled his torso with her thighs. The rhythm of her movements in the moonlight drove any other comparative thoughts from his mind. Gladly relinquishing any further claim to reality, always dutiful Peter gave himself over completely into her exuberant ardor.

"And all the soft moonlight seems to shine in your blush," Van whispered knowingly from the reel-to-reel.

With the morning, they malingered there amongst the sheets, neither one wishing to break the spell. Peter was afraid to open his eyes and find that it had all been a dream. When his searching fingers found her bare shoulder, he sighed a sigh of relief.

Dreams do come true.

Saoirse, on the other hand, felt a tremble of trepidation. Sure, she'd just had an exhilarating romp with a much younger man who seemed to absolutely adore her, but Saoirse knew she was not in love with our dear Peter. Though there had to be some strong feelings, for at least the memory of him, as this was not her usual way. Intimacy of this nature was always a long way in coming for her, brokered slowly over time and moulded through the sweet sensibilities of mutual respect. Peter's sublime passion definitely came from a place deep within him, for Saoirse could feel his sweet restraint, knowing that he was savoring every moment of their in all likelihood limited time together - as if he knew too that this was a one-time thing.

A resounding knock at the front door shook them both back into the present. Once the curtain of surprise had been raised and apprised, there was the obligatory scramble for clothing, with Peter happily flinging Saoirse's red bra across the room for her to hurriedly put on. Then, in the midst of the chaos, they caught each other's eyes. She offered a twinkling thank you for his having stolen away her loneliness. He, a wide-eyed acknowledgment of both grateful love received and her unfettered freedom granted.

It was my lovely Lorraine at the front door. She hadn't been able to connect with Saoirse over the phone, so on the spur of the moment, she decided to drive up unannounced to the old homestead. By all accounts, our dear niece was up there all alone and would no doubt enjoy a bit of loving company.

Though slightly run down, Lorraine thought the old Moose Lake house still looked rather inviting. Although, she'd have to get after Boyd Breedlove about trimming Saoirse's shrubbery. There wasn't much room in the driveway, for there were already two cars lined up there. The old Jeep gave her pause at first, for she didn't recognize it. Was she interrupting something? That feeling quickly faded when she considered the long early morning ride up to the mountains she'd just endured - plus that damn cup of tea her kidneys had so thoroughly processed along the way. Whoever it was that was visiting would have to accept the randomness of fate and the grateful emptying of bladders.

"Anyone to home?" she called out through the front door.

"I'm here Lorraine. Just give me a few... ."

Saoirse looked at Peter as if to say, "what do we do now? How do we explain your being here this early in the morning?"

In answer to her implied question, Peter simply walked over, opened the front door and invited Lorraine in.

"Peter! What a lovely surprise!" Along with her unbridle joy, Lorraine's expression also clearly indicated that she was busily processing all of the possibilities as to how these two young people had arrived in the same place, when they'd both previously inhabited totally different spheres in the universe. They hadn't even seen each other at the extemporaneous gatherings that Lorraine had thrown together when I suddenly passed away. Due to circumstances beyond either of their control, separate viewings had to be scheduled for each of them. I was glad they both made the effort. "Come here Peter," Lorraine gently commanded, "and give your dear old auntie a hug."

Dutiful Peter did as he was told, and when my darlin' wife smelled Saoirse's unique perfume in the boy's hair, she knew everything.

"What's brought you here so early?" Saoirse asked as politely as she could, still fumbling with the buttons on her blouse.

"First, what's my dear boy doing here... without even having bothered to tell me he was on the East Coast again?"

"I just heard about pop's death and I wanted to see the old homestead again," Peter shyly explained. "I guess I needed to be here in this place to know that it was actually true."

"Atwell's gone?" Saoirse sadly asked. "Why didn't you tell me?"

"I'm still processing it all, and besides, I didn't want to spoil the joyous mood of our reunion."

It's makes me smile to absolute no end to think that even in death, old Atwell could spoil the mood. It's what he was best at in life. Later, I'll explain, even though we've both transmogrified to the other side, why I've never seen him haunting anyone. That's funny too, because he was so damn good at haunting folks while he was alive.

"I too was sorry to hear about poor Atwell," Lorraine whispered. "You should have called me and then you wouldn't have had to go home so all alone."

"Thanks Lorraine, but it's all done now. I said my goodbyes and I'm feeling much better about it all. Bumping into Saoirse last night has made a world of difference already."

"I bet she has," Lorraine replied, with a knowing twinkle in her eye. "Did you know Saoirse was living here?"

"Nope. Just a very happy accident."

"He was actually looking for you... ."

"Mostly just a place to spend the night," Peter clarified, with a quick glance at Saoirse - her beauty still beguiling him. "For some reason, all the motels on Route 30 were full-up."

"So, Auntie," Saoirse wondered again. "What's got you up the mountain so early on a Monday morning?"

"I've got a project that I need your kind assistance with... ."

"What kind of project?"

"Oh. The good kind - full of research and writing," Lorraine brightly answered.

Then, after a very necessary bathroom break, and another cup of tea (gratefully prepared by Peter), Lorraine proceeded to tell them how she'd come across those four splendid canvases now hanging in our Nutting house and her desire to learn more about their mysterious creators.

"I could certainly look into this for you?" Saoirse offered, with great interest. The germ of an idea for a book on these individuals was already forming in her brain.

PART FOUR

The first of Lorraine's four artists that Saoirse agreed to investigate was a talented fellow named Raphael Jon Dominic - an Italian, who'd been born the son of a gardener in the Campania region of Southern Italy in 1893. He's the one who'd painted the stylized woman in front of a tree. The family of four had emigrated to the United States when Raphael was just two. His gardener father, Raffaele Cadorna Dominic, who would eventually become a well known landscape architect, no doubt passed on some of his artistic skills to his son. For even at an early age, his passion for sketching the various birds that he saw in his father's gardens led him gladly into the world of Art. In 1911, with an ever growing interest to create, Raphael enrolled in Alfred University's School of Art and Design - the campus is just 200 miles west of Lorraine's and my Nutting house. Following his graduation and the untimely death of his father, Raphael moved west to Berkley, California - hoping to be a comfort to his equally grieving sister. While there he took graduate classes at the California School of Design, now known as the San Fransisco Art Institute.

The Panama-Pacific International Exposition of 1915 exposed Raphael to many previously unknown and original paintings by the likes of Claude Monet, Oskar Kokoschka, Edvard Munch, but most importantly, the Italian Futurists: Umberto Boccioni and Carlo Carrà.

Futurism, with its celebration of advanced technology and urban modernity, is considered by many to be the most important Italian avant-garde art movement of the 20th century. It's energetic members were committed to demonstrating the beauty of modern life and desired to eliminate the need for traditional forms of culture. They fully embraced the grace and elegance of the machine, its speed, its violence, and its ability to create change.

Always a visualist, when World War I caused him to enlist, Raphael joined the U.S. Army Signal Corps, which was based in Maryland at Camp Meade. This location, being so close to Washington D.C. allowed him easy access to the National Art Gallery and its Ninety-third Annual Exhibition of the National Academy of Design. He was obviously taken with the 1918 Hallgarten Prize winner Leopold Seyffert's *The Lacquer Screen*. Saoirse could easily see how inspirational elements from Seyffert's work found their way into Lorraine's found painting. The vibrant interplay of colours in the lacquer screen behind

Seyffert's laconic nude has a very similar look to that of Raphael Dominic's stylized female portrait.

After the Second World War, expanding his range a bit, Dominic began experimenting, choosing to take his now constant landscapes into a more abstract style. This series of works not only showed his deep respect for his dear departed father's love of the land, they also showcased his continued belief in Futurism - that nature is alive, imbued with an energy all its own.

During the 30's and 40's, Raphael roamed the Oregon mountains, sketching and painting vistas along the Columbia River. Still relatively unknown, he began receiving some recognition at regional shows, eventually gaining space for his work in small galleries.

In 1959 he returned to Alfred University, where he taught painting, until he developed untreatable hemorrhages in both eyes which left him legally blind. Thankfully, his love of abstract painting allowed him, even with limited vision to continue to create beautiful landscapes - if only from within his own vivid memories of those Oregon mountains he loved so.

It struck Saoirse then that I too went blind at the end of my artistic life. She wondered, as often did I, whether Raphael and I might have overused our precious sense - wearing our beloved cones of colour down to nubs from constant use.

Michael Bruno, Lorraine's second found artist, was a bit of a surprise, what with his turning out to be a rather talented woman. Something about her signature had thrown Lorraine's auctioneer off his game. Known for her powerful yet elegant work, Michelle Louisa Bruno was a full-blooded Surrealist - greatly inspired by her favorite painter René Magritte. Lorraine's painting, you'll recall, actually had a shadowy Magritte-like figure at the center of its composition.

Like Raphael Dominic's Futurism, Surrealism was also a cultural movement that had developed organically around 1917 - mostly out of the Dada (Anti-Art) crowd's activities. Its aim was to *resolve the previously contradictory conditions of dream and reality.* You no doubt remember me mentioning Marcel Duchamp as being a leading Dadist. Artists like Magritte and Salvador Dali painted disconcerting and often illogical scenes, but with a realistic almost photographic precision. Dali for example would create strange creatures from everyday objects - like dripping clocks and pachyderms with Euphonium heads. Through their art, these artists hoped to allow the unconscious mind to openly express itself.

Michelle came late to the Surrealist party having been born in 1923, nearly twenty years after its start. Its influence on her art grew out of her having spent six years in Paris as a teenager while visiting her Uncle Moreau (a security guard at the Musee d'Orsay). When WWII started and the Germans could be heard in the streets below her windows announcing that Paris was now under curfew, it had to be overwhelming. The horrors she witnessed during the German occupation would return, both in her paintings and ever-present soul-sucking depression.

Just before returning to New York City, Michelle encountered an American painter named Louise Brann who was on a traveling scholarship to study at the Fontainebleau. It was by Louise's suggestion that Bruno enrolled at the city's Cooper Union's School of Art.

During the mid-50s, Bruno, disillusioned by her continued and undiluted anonymity, began to embrace the existential writings of Frenchmen Jean-Paul Sartre and Albert Camus. Their themes of alienation and *angst in the face of the human condition* not only effected her art, they also overpowered her fragile psyche. Sensing the full weight of the absolute *absurdity* of life, along with her impenetrable feelings of sheer loneliness, Michelle ultimately committed suicide at the age of 75 in 1998 - the same age that her philosophical hero Jean-Paul Sartre had died. *"Life has no meaning,"* Sartre books had told her, *"the moment you lose the illusion of being eternal."*

I've always thought it was odd that Sartre himself had never acted on that suicidal conclusion, seeing how he died *naturally* in old age from a pulmonary edema.

Reading about Michelle Bruno's suicide and thinking about Peter's father's recent death, brought Saoirse to a sad place - as her own father, my brother Vincent, had committed the same selfish act. Sure, I saved him that night in the snow when he made his first attempt to rid the world of himself. Vincent's naked run into the frigid wilderness - as if he were wading out into the arms of an ever enveloping ocean - would have worked perfectly had it not been for my hapless intervention. That attempt at usurping death's cruel hand only served to make his life all that much harder. The frostbite to his fingers effectively killed his career as a concert violinist - and that was the only thing in this world that he truly cared about. Saoirse tried to help him through his grief and loss, but though he had good intentions about reconnecting with his daughter, Vincent didn't have that ability. He'd spent far too much of his life thinking only of himself. So, when he finally succeeded at taking his own life, it was as it should be. After all, it was always all about him. His arrogant choice of jumping out that window, without the least bit of concern for any innocent bystanders who might be strolling down below him, was pure egotistical Vincent.

When I put it all together, it seemed ironic that Vincent should choose to step out of a window knowing full well that our own father was killed by a falling crate. There the Milkman was happily walking down the street, minding his own business, probably whistling a happy tune, when a large box, tossed or simply let loose from a high-rise flattened him on a New York City street. Vincent's self-serving free-fall might have done the same thing to some unsuspecting family. Thankfully, when the once grand concert violinist flung himself into the abyss, he kissed that deadly pavement all alone, as there were no hapless victims standing below to catch him.

Why he couldn't find love in his heart for his darling daughter I can't say. Having only two sons myself, dear Saoirse became my beloved daughter. Who else could I have bought all those frilly dresses for? Surely Michael and Eugene would have balked at receiving such feminine gifts. Seeing her at both Vincent's and my funerals told me clearly that I was her favorite father-figure. It saddens me now to recall the tears she wept at my passing, but makes me sadder still that Saoirse had none at all to weep for my misguided brother. Her tears for him, I know all too well, were shed during those many years of anguished absences that she endured while he chose to live outside her gentle sphere.

Now, how about some good news?

It turns out that Paul Henry, Lorraine's third artist, was once the best known painter in all of Ireland during the 20s and 30s. If its provenance proves true, his modest portrait of the woman standing amongst the wooden columns was a lost gem, valued now at €68000 ($77,168.44). That sum alone would repay Lorraine three-fold the purchase price for all four of her found pieces.

Born in Belfast in 1877, Henry studied painting at both the Académie Julian and with American James Abbott McNeill Whistler while in Paris. Whistler, greatly respected, had painted his famous portrait of his mother six years before Henry was even born.

In 1903, he married a Scottish painter named Emily Grace Mitchell. It is her painting of the "Girl in White" from 1910 that Saoirse thought might have inspired Henry's painting in Lorraine's collection. Both husband and wife were famous for painting the western landscapes of Ireland, so these rare portraits really stood out. While Paul was far better known, Grace Henry is considered by some to have been a much more daring painter than her husband. This was due to her free incorporation of many of the new modernist techniques, where he'd stopped experimenting with his own style once they moved to Dublin from their first home together on Achill Island.

Sadly, Paul and Grace divorced in 1929. His second wife, a Brit named Mabel Young (also a landscape painter - working in the impressionistic style) had been his grateful student and eventual lover (before she knew he was married). Only after Grace's death in 1953, would Mabel agree to marry Paul.

I've been to the hills of Ireland, and I can see well why all three of these artists decided to stay there and paint their landscapes. To this day, I'm not even sure why I ever came home again and left those fine emerald hills of my dear father's father.

As Saoirse closed her reference book on the Underground Railroad, she contemplated Lorraine's last auctioned artifact. It's artist, Jefferson Mills Wait was actually a local boy, having been deposited here in the Adirondacks by his freed-slave father.

Father "Otis" was born into slavery on a Lynchburg, Virginia plantation in 1845. Fearing that his older brother Clayton would soon be sold, he stole what was left of his scattered family away, taking the Underground Railroad north at just 16 in 1861 - venturing here to the Adirondacks under the guidance of his resourceful Uncle Pike. That freedom railroad didn't have Pullman Cars and porters. It was more philosophical than that - consisting mostly of a human desire to help enslaved folks get to the Northern states where owning such "living-property" was illegal.

I've always wondered where Lynchburg got its name. Was it really because John Lynch settled there in 1757 while the Native-Americans weren't looking? Or was it because when folks of colour decided to take back their stolen lives, Virginia slave-owners hung them from trees to teach 'em a lesson?

Knowing that men with dogs would be pursuing them, the Waits only traveled at night, keeping off the main roads, and crossing as many streams as possible. "*Water,*" Uncle Pike had said, "*was a masterly mystery to a hound's nose. There's far too many smells in a ramblin' river for 'em to sort through.*"

On occasion, a single lantern beam could be seen, shattering the darkness. That, they'd learned early on, was a signal from some enlightened "conductor" or "stationmaster" that their barn or farmhouse was a safe place to find food and get out of the cold for a spell. They made many stops before choosing to settle in the Speculator area. Uncle Pike, fearing that bounty hunters or slave catchers might come even that far north and steal him away again, decided to continue further on into Canada. *"Ottawa is too far for any Overseer to want to walk and catch an old man like me,"* Uncle Pike had reasoned. At just 43, their Uncle was considered old for a slave. Christ, with an average antebellum life expectancy of just 22 years, both Otis and Clayton were fairly ancient creatures too.

A potter and craftsman by desire, Father Otis did whatever laboring he could find to support his new family - taking on work all over Essex County. He even spent time in North Elba (near Lake Placid) fixing famed Abolitionist John Brown's roof - which he wouldn't take any renumeration for - in solemn tribute to the fallen martyr.

John Brown had moved to North Elba in 1849 when an acre of land cost just $1, hoping to lead freed slaves into farming. The abolitionist Gerrit Smith of Peterboro (a friend of Brown's) offered up some of his Adirondack land (a settlement called Timbuctoo) to black men in a desire to satisfy the "landowning" voting requirement. Brown only lived there for two years before moving to join his concerned sons down in Kansas, where they were fighting ever-expanding pro-slavery factions. Their actions at Harpers Ferry would end in Brown being tried in the Virginia State Court and hung for both murder and treason. Was he a heroic martyr as Father Otis believed or American's first homegrown terrorist? Perhaps Republican Diplomat Frederick Douglass answered that best, when he offered: "*his zeal in the cause of my race was far greater than mine—it was as the burning sun to my taper light—mine was bounded by time, his stretched away to the boundless shores of eternity. I could live for the slave, but he could die for him.*"

Father Otis died before reaching the age of 50 in 1892 - leaving three children: Ophelia, Reeves, and the youngest, Jefferson (1890 - 1953). Though only two when his father passed, young Jefferson was greatly influenced by his father's folk-style art which his mother proudly displayed throughout their modest home. He tried to be a potter like his dad, but found far easier expression through painting.

Now, all this falls directly into line with Lorraine's found painting's history which is dated 1932 - right about the time that Jefferson Wait was creating his first impressionistic works.

Much of what Saoirse was able to find out about Otis Wait and his family was due to Jefferson's biography of his father titled *North to Elba*. For most victims of slavery, freed or otherwise, not much is known outside of scattered census records and passed down word-of-mouth recollections. The book was long out of print, but Saoirse "knows a guy" who "knows a guy" and was able to secure a tattered copy. Being considered only a painter, most critics didn't see Jefferson Wait as a credible author. How could any man be both visually and scholarly elucidative they wondered? I found his written work to be both thoroughly engaging and as visually enticing as his art. Whether it be by brushstroke or pen, his words brought vivid pictures of his father's life easily into my crowded mind.

Some of the quotes I just offered are first hand accounts, coming from Uncle Pike himself. He's a lovely man, with burnt sienna eyes and a gentle manner. He and I had a pleasant chat a year or so ago just south of Washington on the banks of the Potomac River in Alexandria, where he told me wonderful tales of their escape. Etherials like Pike and me enjoy looking at water for some reason. Perhaps it's a manifestation of the ancient Jewish concept of immersion - which makes sense, seeing as how both Pike and I, even though we died a hundred years apart, were both still in the midst of experiencing our end-of-life changes. Remember, time is relative. By their flowing nature, living waters tends to wash away and cleanse us of our past. Something the living should embrace as well.

"Jeezam Crow!" Lorraine said using her vibrant Adirondack slang, for she was astonished by what Saoirse was able to find regarding her four paintings. "You've hit the motherlode."

Unfortunately, none of the artists were still living, so her desire to help them succeed in the world fell stillborn. On the other hand, the monetary value of the Henry canvas alone could certainly repay her initial expenditure, but, like the art lover I so adored, she opted to keep the piece hanging on our wall and forego the profiteering. When her time came to join me, Lorraine's will would provide for both the poor and disenfranchised.

"There's enough information on Jefferson Wait alone for me to write an entire book about him," Saoirse replied happily, glad at having a new writing project.

"Jefferson Wait intrigues me too," Lorraine said, looking up from the report. "If he's a local lad like you say he is, any idea where he might be buried?

"I recall reading that he was laid to rest somewhere near Speculator in the early-50s," Saoirse replied. "On our side of Thomas McMahon's property I believe."

"Didn't that parcel get sold recently... ?"

"I'm not sure, but I can certainly find out." Then Saoirse paused before adding, "wouldn't Boyd Breedlove know that kind of information... ?"

"I'm not sure that I could ask him," Lorraine offered sheepishly. "I just fired him."

"Why would you do that?"

"Two reasons. One, he's been drinking too much lately and shirking his responsibilities around here. Have you seen the shabby state of the shrubbery?"

"And number two?" Saoirse prompted, not really concerned with the landscaping.

"To give our Peter a good reason to stay around," Lorraine answered with a smile. "I've taken the liberty of asking him to look after your property... at least until you're more up and around on that knee."

"It would be nice having him underfoot for a while," Saoirse replied, even as she thought to herself, "but certainly a complication considering what happened the first night he arrived."

Despite what you may think, their agreeable adventure under the sheets hadn't had a reoccurrence, mostly because both parties recognized the singularity of their shared emotions. He'd happily fulfilled a long-held desire to make love to a once unobtainable holy grail, and she'd experienced the pleasure of some much needed adoration and compassion. For now, just being in each other's company, while holding that shared memory was enough. But, just to make sure things didn't get out of hand again, Peter had moved out to a motel.

"I've also arranged for Peter to stay at Morgan Sullivan's place," Lorraine, ever the consummate planner explained. "While Morgan is in the hospital, someone has to look after his chickens."

"And that would be Peter?"

"The boy knows stuff," Lorraine replied.

"He certainly does... ." Saoirse agreed with a mischievous smile.

The next morning Saoirse stopped by the county clerk's office and asked to examine the McMahon property's public records. The 72-acre parcel had indeed just been bought by Donald Kallstadt, a wealthy land developer from Philadelphia. His plan, according to the file on record was to build a hotel complex with an adjacent water park. Just what the Adirondacks needed.

Looking closely at an 1888 survey map included in the packet, she could just make out a small house and a cemetery icon near the far southern border, not far from her own property line.

The following day, Peter drove Saoirse out to the far edge of her property in his CJ5. An ebullient wind blew through and around the Jeep's old canvas top, smelling of early morning rain and pungent pine. To his delight, the breeze was playfully tossing Saoirse's ponytail on and then off her enticingly slender neck. Beauty was everywhere. All you had to do was notice it. The macadam road ended a thousand yards from where the cemetery should be, so he paused a moment to switch-out the wheel hubs into four-wheel-drive.

"Don't let me forget to switch these babies back before we hit the highway again."

"I'll try," Saoirse replied as they crept slowly through the underbrush.

Oddly, there seemed to be a haphazard path previously blazed before them. Like the power company or some such crew had had reason to enter the woods some months before. Ahead of them, they could see a clearing leading up to a fine vista. She could easily see why Kallstadt wanted to put a hotel near here. His customers would be forever clamoring to get one of the scenic-view rooms.

"I'm going to need to paint that view before the hotels go up," Peter said, more to himself than out loud. He could envision the composition almost immediately, which was always a good sign.

"Shouldn't that 'terry be right there?" Saoirse asked as she pointed to a set of newly placed property markers.

"You'd think so. At least, based on that old property map."

Then, out of the corner of his eye, Peter noticed an odd shaped slope in the landscape. Nature, he knew from years of observation, wouldn't have polished the hillside that abruptly, so he chose to take a closer look.

"It seems like somebody dumped some land-fill here... ."

"On my property?"

"Yep," Peter answered as he walked back towards Kallstadt's new property line. "And that's where the debris came from." Well beyond the new flapping hot-pink markers, Peter could see the remains of a stone foundation and an equally odd depression in the soil - maybe thirty or forty feet square. "Based on these faded caterpillar tracks, it looks to me like somebody took a payloader in there and flipped out the dirt from that depression over onto your property."

"Why the hell would anybody do that?"

"Maybe to move a historic cemetery... ?"

"Then Kallstadt, the bastard, didn't want anything to get in the way of his fucking fun park!"

"Yep." Peter agreed, as he held up the top half of a century-old tombstone that he'd pulled out of the debris pile.

"We can't leave it like this... ."

"Who's to say exactly when this earth got disturbed, or if those graves were ever really on Kallstadt's property?"

"I'll take care of it," Saoirse replied. "Those folks deserve much better than being so thoughtlessly uprooted and dumped like that. Even if the courts decided in our favor, Kallstadt would never do right by them. So, I will."

No one would have probably ever known that this switch in burial plots had ever taken place if my dear Lorraine hadn't decided to purchase those paintings in the first place. Needing to know things, like where Jefferson Wait was buried, was always her best quality. No. That's not accurate. Lorraine's sweet kisses were her best attribute, and I should know, she gave me plenty of them - and always out of her own free will.

Before leaving the site, Peter took multiple photographs of the burial debris field, the disturbed section of Kallstadt's property, and just for himself, a few of that splendid Adirondack view. He'd definitely be back soon with his brushes and a canvas.

"We need to determine which body belongs to which stone?" Saoirse said, as the Jeep hit the main road again, "before we can resurrect all the monuments correctly."

"We'll need a forensic expert to help with that," Peter offered, "seeing how all the stones and bones are all mixed-up together now."

"Did you remember to switch those wheel thingies!?" Saoirse asked, suddenly panicked, fearing that one of the old Jeep's wheels might pop off.

"Yep," Peter replied nonchalantly. "I did it while you were off trying to call Lorraine."

"Damn mountains. I can never get cell service anywhere up here."

"Some folks call that a vacation."

Three telephone calls later, and Saoirse found herself speaking directly to Rhetta (Rita) Cockerell, a forensic archeologist formally with the New York State Museum at the Capital. It was an easy decision for Rhetta, now a private contractor, to get onboard - especially after she heard what had happened. She wasn't the least bit surprised, just annoyed. Kallstadt wasn't the first thoughtless real estate scoundrel that she'd encountered in her twelve years of careful human excavation and analysis.

Early the next week, Rhetta found herself in the Adirondacks for the first time. The ride up from Redden was uneventful. She'd hoped to spy a moose meandering across Route 8, as she'd long to see one in the wild her entire life, but only the occasional deer and woodchuck greeted her ascent. Though this world of trees and streams was far outside her normal urban haunts, she found the endless solitude refreshing. No. There were no radio talk show hosts trying to make her angry. No honking horns criticizing or condemning her driving style. And...no angry cab drivers sparring with their metal bumpers, looking to challenge and reclaim her space in the downtown traffic lanes.

When Saoirse saw Rhetta coming up the walkway she marveled at the woman's wonderful tangle of rasta braids as they tossed this way and that. She was taller than Saoirse by a head and, as they gladly shook hands, she found herself envying the tone of the younger woman's youthful auburn skin. Even while dressed in ripped cargo pants, orange chukka boots, and a faded blue denim work shirt, Rhetta Cockerell was a knock-out.

The kitchen table had been commandeered for this meeting, and was completely covered with maps and drawings - mostly of the McMahon property.
After the women discussed Saoirse and Lorraine's plans for reclaiming the cemetery, Rhetta suggested that they drive over to the site so that she could see the situation first hand.

"Shall I drive, or shall you?" Saoirse asked as they walked out to the driveway again. The cast had been removed from her knee and only a brace could be seen beneath her olive slacks.

"Why don't I," Rhetta suggested. "You may know the way and all, but I have a trunk full of tools."

They spent the rest of the afternoon there working the site, leaving only when darkness made it too difficult to see. The cemetery had certainly been moved, and without any concern for the folks who'd been laid to rest there.

"It's going to take some time to sort out all the players," Rhetta said.

"We figured that," Saoirse replied. "But don't worry about being paid. My benefactor Lorraine is gladly footing the bill."

Rhetta wasn't worried about the money. She felt so strongly about doing the right thing for these discarded people, she'd have done it all for nothing.

The next morning, two distinctively different things happened - but which were actually very much the same when you look back at the specific details. I know that sounds confusing, but as I've previously stated, I now see time in arcs of 360 degrees - future and past all at the same instant. The only real difference being, that while I'm not always surprised by what's about to happen, the painful part is not being able to do a damn thing to stop or enhance it.

Thing #1: It was just after sunrise when Peter decided to drive out to the McMahon property vista and begin painting his landscape. At least to get an initial sketch together, so that he could complete the canvas later on in Sullivan's barn. The chickens may even enjoy seeing a different view of the world for a change - and who wouldn't?

Walking in nature took additional time for Peter - like reading a book, where the reader gets caught on the shape of the very words and letters. Seeing any landscape made him stop and wonder about its possible compositions. His vivid landscapes captured the viewer's eye - not only keeping it within the frame of the canvas, but requiring them to pull up a lawn chair so that they could remain in that moment for hours. It's a skill that I wish I could say that I taught him, but I didn't. Nobody did. He just owns it, like the colour of his eyes.

Not wishing to disturb the gravesite any more than it'd been already, Peter opted to walk his gear through the woods and into the clearing. It took only a few minutes to set up his easel, and get the canvas properly placed. He looked out at the vista, knowing he'd chosen the best possible time of day to be there. The sun was just high enough in the sky to cast gentle shadows across the vista's floor.

Even with all his experience, Peter, to my way of thinking, was not accessing the best possible view of his prima sunlit panorama. There was something, not yet seen that he might miss and I'd hate for that to happen. So, though limited as my powers are to change anything in the living world, I blew a soft redolent breath towards the westward side of his face causing him to turn his head ever-so-slightly in my direction. I chose the smell of honeysuckle from my boundless scent palette for two reasons. One, it was always Siobhán's favorite, and two, because it would offer a compelling divergence from the normally overwhelming smell of pine and might catch his attention. Now, thanks to my wee subtle stunt, he was looking where he could see everything - including his future.

As he busily sketched the lines of the composition with a new stick of charcoal, he looked out at the view, and not at the canvas. He let his hand flow freely across the white horizontal plane, not concerning himself with an exact duplication of what actually existed in the panorama, but a more impressionistic view. The freedom of his movements always made me so envious, for Peter seemed to interact directly with his muse, while I often stumbled amongst its minutiae.

As he worked the lines of the nearest rim, he noticed a bump in the arc that he hadn't noticed before. Then it was gone. Then it returned and was gone again.

"What the hell?" he mumbled, as he recognized what appeared to be a head bobbing up and down before him. "Hello?"

"Hello yourself," the bobbing head replied, sounding rather annoyed. "Am I in your way?" she added sarcastically.

"No. Not really."

When Rhetta stood up and identified herself, Peter couldn't look way.

Now, you've no doubt heard the term "thunderstruck" before. It's cliche, certainly, but ofttime there's no better word for it. Well, this wasn't his simply being *extremely surprised or shocked* by something. It was Peter falling in love. If you had listened closely enough, you could of heard his guard being completely let down, his hopes broadening exponentially, his desires engorging, and his heart opening as wide as humanly possible. Yeah. I know there are sour-puss skeptics out there who can't begin to believe such a thing occurs, but it can happen that way. When I first met my dear Siobhán I too was thunderstruck - both by her beauty and the idea of forever. Maybe it's our artistic temperament that allows us to see an immediate future with someone. Or, maybe it's simply a self-delusion brought about by an overly romantic mind. At any rate. dear, dutiful Peter very much *liked* what he saw rising surprisingly from the ashes.

Rhetta had a totally different take. While she found Peter's countenance pleasant enough, he was rudely interrupting her. She was busily working after all. Christ, by her last count, she had nearly ten people looking up from the dirt and relying on her to get this right. Though, interesting as this stalwart fellow might be, given the stunned look in his manly artist's eyes, she had no time for such an Adirondack romance.

"Oh! You're the forensic archeologist that Saoirse hired."

"That's me," she replied trying not to sparkle. I get how it's hard for a gem like Rhetta not to shine, especially when her natural beacon is so bright. "Now, if you'll excuse me, I've got folks here waiting for me to sort them out."

"I won't bother you if I continue sketching?"

"I can't see how you could - any more than you already have... ."

When Peter had completed his sketching (and he did a splendid job by-the-way), he walked quietly over to where Rhetta was shifting dirt through a square wooden screen. He didn't say a word for the longest time, not wishing to disturb her work. The determined archaeologist didn't seem to notice him at all, but simply went about her digging and thinking with the conviction of a seasoned professional. Just standing there, observing her was distraction enough. Peter enjoyed watching her strong hands as they moved confidently about separating the earth from its long slumbering and no longer suffering silent dwellers.

When she finally looked up at him, Peter asked, "that's how you separate the bones from the soil? With that screen?"

"It catches most of the pieces," Rhetta replied. "It's slow going, but there's really no other way."

"Couldn't you use a bigger shovel instead of that tiny spade?"

"In Archaeology, the smaller the tool the better," she replied, no longer looking up. "Otherwise you tend to get the same shitty results as this asshole real estate developer got."

"Could I help you... somehow?"

"There's not much room down here - it's already pretty crowded."

"It's in my nature. I've got to be useful," he pleaded. Then, under his breath he added, "Especially to you."

"I suppose you could act as transportation."

"Carrying stuff. Yeah. I could be that."

As the sunset began gathering momentum and there was no escaping the approaching darkness, Peter asked, "how'd you get here? I didn't see a car up on the road."

"Saoirse dropped me off," Rhetta replied, looking a little concerned. Then after checking her watch, she added anxiously, "she was supposed to be here to retrieve me over an hour ago."

"Somethin' must have come up," Peter offered. He would later learn that he'd reasoned correctly. "Why don't you let me drive you back to her house."

"Transportation! Exactly what I assigned you to do?"

"Yep," dutiful Peter replied as he helped Rhetta gather up her boxes of bones, tombstones, and tools.

"Nice CJ5 you've got there," Rhetta said as they exited the clearing. "What year is it?"

"1958 Willy's," Peter replied too proudly. "It once belonged to my father."

"Mine's a '76 Wagoneer. It used to belong to Bob's Uscd Cars."

It's my thought that due to a gene for natural selection, when a man sees a group of women, he instantly sorts through them, looking for those attributes that might best further his own bloodline.

Not that this is even a conscious thing. Just something that happens on both sides of the gender fence - as I'm certain that women find themselves doing it too. He might look for childbearing hips while she's attracted to strength and stability. My point here is that there were many elements in Rhetta that Peter's dutiful gene pool found exciting. After thousands of years of evolution, he simply couldn't turn away from their insistent siren's call hoping to obtain the best adaptation to the environment. Falling for Rhetta was therefore inevitable... especially if the Phillips line were ever to survive the new millennia. Crusty old Atwell had put a pretty bad hurtin' on the family's heredital pond, and unconsciously Peter's wretched DNA was hoping against hope to finagle a little classy genetical spackling.

Thing #2: Earlier, even as Peter's Jeep was leaving the driveway, a vintage Ford Fairlane was pulling up to the Moose Lake house. You see, Saoirse was also about to be *thunderstruck*, only this time by someone she'd never expected to see again.

The knocking on the kitchen door seemed to be coming from far away. It was relentless in its gentle persistence. Saoirse adjusted her knee brace, stood up, and walked slowing toward the sound. The black car in the driveway didn't look familiar, so she switched her reaction meter from curious to cautious. She was a woman living alone after all.

When she saw Chord Murtagh's redoubtable face so sweetly framed by the kitchen door's red-picnic-table-plaid curtains, she almost laughed.

"What are you doing here?" she yelled through the door, as she slowly returned to anger.

"Can Ah come in?" he pleaded. "I've got much tae say, that works best if it's nae bein' filtered by a damn door."

"What's the point!?"

"There's things that Ah need tae say fur mah own mental health, whether ye want tae hear'em ur not."

"All right then," she replied, as she absentmindedly flipped the always opened lock, locking the door.

"Ah cannae gie in," Chord protested, as he tried the door.

"Oh... damn it."

With the lock now unlocked, Chord pushed open the door. She was a little disappointed that he wasn't wearing his kilt, but that feeling shifted 180 degrees after she reached over and slapped him hard across the face.

"Ah hope that made ye feel better," he said, as his cheek burnt red where she'd struck him.

"I don't know. Come closer and maybe I'll do it again."

"I'm sure that Ah deserved that. Yoo've a perfect reason tae be angry wi' me."

"You think...?"

"First, lit me say that I'm sorry."

"Sorry for what? Breaking my fucking heart?"

"Yes... an' fur nae tellin' ye th' whole truth."

"A liar and a heartbreaker," Saoirse replied, with a wee touch of whimsy. "What else do you do? Drown cats?"

"Ah apologize, an' Ah changed," Chord answered firmly, the look in his eyes clearly indicating that he thoroughly meant what he'd just said.

"OK. I've got ten minutes. Explain yourself."

"Shooldn't we go tae anither room? Maybe one wi' fewer knives in it?"

"No. I'd hate for you to get too comfortable. I allowed you that luxury for two years in my apartment and see where that got me."

"Please hear me out, if ye don't like what I've come tae say, ye can fling me erse out for good an' always."

"You have nine minutes... ."

"It was all Claire's idea - mostly," Chord began, "her an' Ah gettin' married Ah mean. It embarrasses me tae say that handfastin' (marriage) with me was somethin' she'd always dreamt of."

"And yet, you've never spoken of her to me before."

"Ah must've. I've known th' McCrimmons all me life - since childhood really. Claire an' Ah waur sort of betrothed back when we waur kids in Culloden (*Cùl lodain*)."

"You'd think that I would recall hearing about a woman you so desperately loved," Saoirse replied. "Especially one that you'd chosen to leave me for!"

"That's not whit happened... ."

"You could have fooled me!"

"Our gettin' married was Claire's desire - not mine," Chord replied,trying not to be argumentative. "Ah only wanted a viable reason fur leavin' ye th' way that Ah did."

"And that reason was... ?"

"Not coz Ah didn't loove ye. Ah do loove ye. Ah still loove ye!"

"Funny way to show it, taking off with another woman like that... ."

He moved in closer and rested his hand on her arm before adding, "Ah was afraid." Saoirse could see that it pained him greatly to admit his fear. "Ah was afraid that Ah wooldn't be th' kin'ay man ye needed... not when it really coonted."

"After two years together, why would you suddenly arrive at that deluded conclusion?"

"Ah was't sure," he answered even more painfully, "that Ah could sufficiently give up me spirits should a bairn (child) arrive atween us. Ye know how I've always loved me drinkin'."

"So, we're back to my having wanted a child... ."

"It's not an easy thin' admittin' yer shortcomin's, especially to th' woman ye loove."

"My desires haven't changed!" Saoirsc snapped back. "So, why have you followed me here?"

"Mah desires have," Chord admitted freely. "Us bein' so far apart - that we're not even talkin' any longer - hurts me in a place so deep that I've ne'er knoon its like afore."

"I know that place," she admitted in a whisper as her eyes met his, which emboldened him to go on.

"When Ah have me mornin' tea, yer cup should be restin' alang side mine. When Ah once again get tae walk alang th' shores of Moray Firth, Ah want yer hand tae be in mine. but most of all, when Ah look across mah wide sorry bed on any night of th' week, Ah want tae see you lyin' thaur beside me."

"That's where we once were," Saoirse replied with tears in her eyes. "And then you chose to leave... ."

"Aye. That Ah did. But I'm a smarter man now, given our impossible separation."

"What are you saying? You're willing to have a child with me now?"

"Aye. That Ah am."

"Are you saying goodbye to alcohol then?"

"Aye. Ah am."

"For me?"

"Nae. Mah loove. Fur me."

Slowly Chord pull Saoirse to him, and after a soft kiss, he added, "drinkin' fur me now is jist a means of killin' th' pain of mah loosin' you. It's jist a drug - a damnable anesthetic that tastes of soor medicine in me mouth. I'd raither be free of it an' have you, raither than 'tother way aroond."

"And a child... ?"

"Ah see it as bein' a wee gift," he offered with a genuine smile. "That way there'd be a bit more of you in th' warld fur me tae loove."

"And a bit more of you for me," Saoirse agreed before returning his soft kiss.

In my time among the living, I've known at least a dozen men who've taken Chord's vow to stop drinking - at least to excess. Most of them were actually successful in keeping that sacred oath. There is a switch in a man's psyche that thoroughly transforms his inner being once his first child is born. If the system is operating correctly, his once manic ego shifts easily from *my, me, mine* to a more euphoric and compelling *his, hers, theirs* without so much as a whisper. Being sober in a time of crisis is like no other gift. It is a moment of divine intervention where a clear mind and purposeful resolve can cure most ills. If the man has so lost his soul and that rocker switch doesn't automatically flip, it becomes a beacon of resounding despair. This is where Saoirse's ex-husband Richard lost his way and is now in prison. Bringing a babe into this world has always meant personal sacrifice - that being the greater part of your life in exchange for a better beginning to their more perfect lives. Foundations are poured with heavy cement for a reason. There will be plenty of time, once they've reached maturity and flown from the nest to tie-on one alcohol-infused bender unto the next.

The same, I'm afraid, goes for tobacco and all means of second-hand smoke. Wouldn't you agree that someone's deadly pleasure should never interfere with the simple act of a child's breathing. I remember my father, Owen, telling my brother Vincent and me about how our Grandfather chose to give up smoking cigars in a single afternoon. Well, it really wasn't his idea, but certainly his choice to comply. At the birth of his first grandchild (Vincent), Grandmother'd told him to stop smoking, simply because of the kids' well-being. Not asked, mind you. Told. Without one single word of argument, Grandpa easily saw the need. His final cigar was toked to a half-inch stub - without anguish - right there at the garden table where he'd smoked for over twenty years. He never once lit up again - at least not in our presence. With due pride in his selfless achievement, I can still imagine how hard that final act really was, for Owen had told us that he could see in his own father's eyes just how much he enjoyed each and every last puff.

"Damn it!" Saoirse shouted, as she hastily looked at her wristwatch. "I've forgotten to pick up Rhetta!"

"Who's Rhetta?" Chord wanted to know, not wishing to unhand his newly recaptured love.

"Stay!" she commanded, giving him a hard look as if the Scotsman were a Cairn Terrier. "I'll be right back!"

Moving much better with the knee brace, Saoirse grabbed her keys and was out the door before her lover could form his next question.

Now, you're askin' yourself, how the hell did Chord Murtagh find Saoirse when she'd hidden herself so carefully in the Adirondacks? Not even a mosquito in full blood-lust could've found her so easily. We're goin' to put the blame for that ease on dear Lorraine. Always a believer in true love, she couldn't stand to see her niece so terribly in pain. So... when Chord sent out feelers to all the folks who might know where his love might've disappeared to, Lorraine happily responded. To his credit, my darlin' wife thought the Scotsman had three things goin' for him: he was an absolutely gorgeous man - both inside and out, he never kicked dogs or folks when they were down, and he was a painter like me.

As Saoirse sped down the highway, she thought about what it might actually mean having Chord back in her life. She'd known he was the *one* from their very first meeting in New York City. It was only because he was born stubborn that it took him this long to see the same light. Hopefully, he was back now for good and always, but she'd be happy if he'd only stayed long enough for the conception of a child. She knew romances could be fickle - depending on the whimsy of both changing circumstance and desire. Therefore, anything after that tiny bit of inception, would all be frosting.

The road around her property was void of any other traffic, so she began to daydream a little. Having Chord back in her life made her think about the first time they met. She was so occupied with her memories, Saoirse didn't even see Peter and Rhetta waving to her as they drove by.

Saoirse, new to the Big Apple and hoping to embrace a free evening's adventure, decided to do the tourist thing and visit the Empire State Building. Not really sure how, but following the directions provide by the guidebook's map, she ventured down the grey concrete steps of the New York City subway hoping to catch the R train with the intention of getting off at the Herald Square Station. The adventure started almost immediately.

Across the tracks on the other side of the station platform she could see a young woman in a bright red party dress walking alone. She seemed confused as to where to be and what to do, as that side of the tracks was temporarily closed to all Manhattan bound trains. The moody Ticketmaster in his dark cubicle was yelling at her at the top of his voice. The animated fellow looked like a Punch and Judy character as he danced and pounded his fists. The Red Woman had no inkling as to why he was acting so angrily.

On Saoirse's side of the tracks, she could see a rugged-looking yet extremely handsome man watching the same situation unfold. As he moved towards the Ticketmaster, she couldn't take her eyes off of his knees. The man's tartan kilt fit him well and told her that maybe he too was a tourist.

"Stop yelling at the puir lass," the Scotsman called out. "She obvioosly doesn't understand why or what yoo're yellin' aboot."

"She can't be over there!" the Ticketmaster cried. "It just can't be done!"

The Red Woman stopped and moved over towards the roped-off turnstiles, hoping to climb over them and onto Saoirse's side of the station. This action sent the little Ticketmaster into even further riotous pangs of vocal anguish.

"Get off them ropes! Get off them ROPES!"

"Tak' it easy thaur, wee fella," the Scotsman cautioned, showing his wide palm at the fellow as though it were a stop sign. "I've got 'er from here." With that the big man took the Red Woman by the hand and gently led her away.

"Thank you kind sir. I can't image why that man was so angry with me."

"You obvioosly stepped outside his norm. Th' wee fellow's bin in that cubical far tay long an' he's jealoos of those who gladly step ootside of their given boondaries."

"Somehow, I got myself on the wrong side of the tracks," she confessed. "All the postings said I should be on that side of the station in order to get down to 47th Street."

"Aye, an' that would be th' case if thaur weren't so mony renovations goin' on," the Scotsman clarified. "Signs donna do a bodie any good if they are no longer relevant tae th' occasion. If ye want tae get tae 47th street from here, yoo're goin' tae have tae ride in th' opposite direction fur a few stations - until we get tae one that's still got access tae th' west boond side."

Saoirse, slightly embarrassed, admitted to having overheard their exchange and asked if she could join the couple as they waited for the next available car. The Scotsman couldn't believe his luck at having a beautiful lass on each arm.

"My name's Saoirse... ."

"A pleasure," the Scotsman replied, really meaning it, for the look in her gentle eyes took him all the way home to Inverness again.

"And I'm Eva Prishtina," The Red Woman offered, along with her grateful hand.

"Chord Murtagh," the Scotsman replied, gladly taking Eva's hand, yet still looking deep into Saoirse's eyes. "Ye from Kosovo?"

"How did you know that?" Eva's look of amazement made her seem even more the innocent lamb.

"I've a wee gift wi' accents," he laughed, as Saoirse reluctantly released him from her gaze. "Actually, me mother is Yugoslavian. Born in Dubrovnik she was."

"That's on the coast, not far from my hometown." His being part Yugoslavian suddenly allowed Eva to trust him, and Chord could easily see that joyful transformation in her eyes.

"Shall I go out on a limb," Saoirse asked, "and guess that you're from Scotland?"

"Aye," Chord admitted. "It's me knees what's given me away. I'm a piper jist comin' aff a rehearsal fur a gig. Braw (nice) as it is, Ah don't always wear me breacan out in public much."

"It's a lovely plaid," the two women's expressions seemed to say as their eyes lingered low.

"Ur you a natife New Yorker then?" Chord asked Saoirse, changing the subject. "Ur a toorist like oorselves?"

"I'm a New Yorker born and bred, just not from The City."

"Upstate ur from th' island?' Chord wanted to know. "It makes a difference."

"Upstate. Just right of the Capital."

"Ah main have a job waitin' fur me up thaur," he offered wistfully. "Too soon tae tell reit now, but it'd be brilliant havin' a friend aroond if Ah do."

"I've just transplanted myself here," Saoirse replied, sensing that they might always be two ships passing.

For reasons that he'd later understand, despite their only having just met, Chord felt an odd pang of sadness at her having chosen to stay in New York City.

When the train finally arrived, Chord allowed the ladies to enter first. There were no empty seats, so the trio stood together near the door. As was his routine, along with locating all possible exits, Chord calmly scanned the interior of the car, looking for anything that might prove troublesome. To his dismay a thoroughly drunken man had already set his deviant sights on the lovely and unsuspecting Eva.

The raggedy fellow, dressed in his official *Punk* uniform, with his sneakers missing their laces and his hair all fanned out in a bright pink Mohawk, was randomly taking sips of alcohol from a dented hip-flask. As if he need to get any drunker.

Chord, sensing this fellow's aberrant desire, chose to stand between he and Eva, essentially blocking the roisterous man's view. Hoping an out-of-sight-out-of-mind policy might be the proper solution.

"Hey! Girly-man!" the drunken Punk called out viciously - obviously taking exception to the Scotsman's traditional attire. Chord chose to ignore him. "I'm talkin' to you Fuckhead!"

Saoirse gave the fellow a hard stare, as she followed Chord's heroic lead, moving herself as well between the drunk and his innocent prey. To counter this, the boisterous man simply leaned forward, nearly kneeling down in the aisle.

"Ain't she the most beautiful fuckin' woman on the fuckin' planet," the drunk asked an eight-year-old boy sitting near by with his father. "Fuckin' beautiful that!"

Chord turned around. Any sober individual would've read the situation correctly, seen the vexation, and stopped right there, but not this guy.

"Get the fuck out of the way Braveheart! You're blockin' my view of paradise!"

"Wa don't ye just sit back an' tak' 'er easy, wee man?"

"I am takin' it easy, asshole. That woman in red is real *easy* on the eyes - if only you'd get your damn skirt outta the way."

Seeing that this idiot was beyond reasonable conversation, Chord simply turned his back again. Why bother to engage this fellow any further? 47th Street was only a few stops away and soon all would return to quiet again.

"What stop are you getting off on," Saoirse asked Eva.

"47th. My sister is meeting me at Jack Dempsey's around 8:30."

"When you get off," Saoirse warned, "be aware of those around you. This asshole might decide to follow you once you're both off the train."

Eva was grateful for the tip. She hadn't even considered his following her.

As the car slowed to a stop, Eva wished them both well and got off as planned on 47th. The drunk had difficulty standing up and missed the stop altogether.

When they were approaching the 42nd Street Station, the drunk got up and stood tipsily behind them. The minute the doors opened he angrily pushed his way by, stopping just long enough on the platform to show Chord his shiny switchblade.

"I'd've cut you Braveheart, except that your girlfriend here is so damn pretty. Wouldn't want to've upset her... unnecessarily."

Saoirse and Chord let the doors close hoping it would draw the final curtain on this farce. When the doors didn't reopen again, Chord and Saoirse continued on to the 34th street station. From there it would only be a couple of blocks walk to the Empire State Building and likely a whole lot safer. The drunken punk might have changed his mind and be lying in wait for them at their present location.

"Can Ah tag along an' visit th' Empire State Buildin' with ye?" Chord asked as they walked arm-in-arm along the 34th Street towards the world-famous skyscraper.

"That would only make the view from the top all that much better," she offered with a winsome smile.

There was something about his heroic nature on the train that brought her immediately back to the vintage black and white movies of her youth. His not being worried about his own personal safety while looking out for Eva was admirable - especially in a world where self-interest seemed to be the fashion of the day. Amidst the Noir New York City landscape of stark light and shadow, the Scotsman seemed the perfect blend of Gary Copper's laconic warrior style and Robert Mitchum's wry good looks.

The view from the then third tallest building in New York City was a spectacular vision of illumination and shadow - especially looking out over the Theater District, only thirteen minutes to the northwest, with all its vibrant marquee lights. Vying too for their attention was both the art-deco Chrysler Building behind them and Madison Square Garden glowing so brilliantly a few blocks to the west.

As Saoirse walked slowly along the red brick observation deck she could see the Hudson River below her on the left. The East River was out of sight somewhere off to her right. Unfortunately, due to a history of some sad folks' misguided ideas, she had to look through quarter-inch thick diamond shaped steel wires to see the sites. Chord, with a much better view in mind, was standing near the elevators watching her. There was a grace to her movements which clearly indicated a perfect blend of both feral femininity and earned confidence.

"Weel? What dae ye think?" Chord asked when she finally wandered over to his little corner of the world. "Worth climbin' aw those fifteen hundred an' seventy-six steps?"

"Most assuredly yes," she replied, glad that they had actually taken an elevator up to the 86th floor. "It's breath taking... ."

"It sure is," Chord agreed, still looking only at her."

"Will you have a drink with me when we both get down to earth again?"

"Sure," he replied with enthusiasm. Though after having met Saoirse he wasn't sure if his feet would ever quite touch terra firma again.

That night, after everyone had returned to the Moose Lake house, Chord and Saoirse quickly excused themselves, leaving Peter and Rhetta alone to get better acquainted. Everyone knew where the recently realigned lovers were going, and Peter, who still cared greatly for his Saoirse, gladly let her go. He simply wanted her to be happy and the Scotsman seemed to be the right catalyst to make that happen. Beside, Peter was developing a new interest in the all-work and no-play archeologist. Like many a man 'afore him - including me-self - a woman's seeming disinterest only fuels the fires of ardor. What you can't *have* easily becomes what you *must* have. So, as the sounds of gentle flirtations in the big bedroom grew to the passionate throws of seasoned love making, Peter offered Rhetta a cup of tea. This was his first step. For his tea was so satisfying that it took away all of a woman's stress - except maybe for any sexual tension, which it only strengthened.

Did you know that unprotected sex can have real consequences?

When little Rose Lyric Murtagh was born eight and a half months later by caesarian section, it would be difficult to say just who the father was. It was another six months or so before her sweet face began to inform on whether she looked more like Peter or the Scotsman.

.

PART FIVE

At first, Rhetta and Peter took the collection of tombstones and bones they'd found back to the Moose Lake house for sorting, but the only available space there to lay everything out was in the old garage. It'd been built in 1909 to house one of Henry Ford's brand new Model T automobiles. The Detroit Piquette Avenue Tin Lizzie was a mechanical wonder, selling over fifteen million units in its eighteen years of production. Unfortunately the vehicle was built more like a high carriage than a current low-slung sedan, coming off the production line both four inches thinner and shorter than even Peter's CJ5 - which most folks today would consider a smallish vehicle. This meant that despite the garage's huge entry door, being exceptionally high at over seven feet tall to accommodate the Ford, the Jeep nor any other modern conveyance would fit inside. Plus, like any other garage in America, it was filled with stuff. Merchandise that an economy based on an ever increasing need for higher and higher annual sales that required its citizens to buy things and even more things - whether they could afford them or not.

Just how many carbon fiber toilet seats, Mariman Monarch Prestigio golf clubs, and Italian leather handbags does any one American need?

Anyway, in Lorraine's garage there was also a full set of summer chairs - with all of the accompanying overstuffed floral cushions that it takes to make the damn things comfortable; a riding lawn mower that she used to love to ride, as well as a snow blower that she hated to operate, and all of the things associated with them; a canoe and all the things connected with that; not to forget dear Lorraine's snowmobile - that she used to save my life - all of which were now buried beneath a dozen boxes filled with stuff we never bothered to move south when we left for Nutting years ago.

When Lorraine noticed the shocking lack of accommodations at Moose Lake, she immediately offered up our Nutting house's garage. In contrast, the new structure was mostly empty and having been built to house parade floats, of all things, was designed to be quite spacious. In fact, the dance-floor-like room was completely unencumbered by those pesky support columns that architects so often require that not only hold up the roof but seem to take up so much damn interior space. The Nutting builders had used special trusses to support the weight of the roof all while minimizing any need for those infernal internal intrusions. In this new space Rhetta and Peter could lay out all of the bones and stones at one time - making it far easier to sort through all of the equally grey and similarly shaped puzzle pieces.

To help with the project, Lorraine borrowed a half-dozen plywood panels and enough saw-horses to support them from a contractor that she knew. Like every other man in her life, he'd fallen in love with her immediately and therefore could deny her nothing.

Ah... the power of women.

"It'll be like trying to put together a eight-hundred piece jig-saw puzzle - when all the pieces are the same cloudy-grey," Peter'd commented. "No colour prompts what-so-ever, leaving us only the edges and corresponding shapes to tell which pieces might fit into another."

"Did I ever tell you that archeology is a slow, pain-staking process?" Rhetta asked rhetorically. She wasn't expecting an answer.

"The word tedious comes to mind," Peter replied, giving her one anyway.

Despite her early dismissal of all things Peter, Rhetta's respect for him was growing daily. He wasn't only a diligent worker, but quite astute regarding all manner of things. Peter's educated hands were quick and agile, as was his first-class mind, and when he made small talk it included comments and quotes from the great masters of not only art, but music and philosophy as well. Above all things, she hated repeating herself, as it not only wasted time but energy. Peter, she was pleased to see, was a fine listener and often had something relevant or insightful to say regarding her work. Pretty men, in her experience, often lacked the necessary intelligence to be both useful and appealing.

"I called a pal of mine back in Santa Fe to ask about how we can best repair the headstones," Peter told her, as they walked into the Nutting house garage together.

"You might've just asked me," Rhetta replied, though she appreciated his initiative.

"Whichever way you prefer," Peter replied. "I'm just happy to help."

"Well, you did a fine job with *transportation*, she uncharacteristically praised him. "Having that tow-ball on your Jeep, not to mention access to a box trailer, made it a lot easier gettin' all these artifacts safely down the mountain."

"My old man got plenty of use out of that old trailer, what with his constant gatherin' of junkyard debris and other worthless salvages over the years. When he was in business, Atwell's old Mercantile sold everythin' - both used and new. He was such a procrastinator though, I'm surprised the damn thing was even licensed much less inspected."

"While I was collectin' the fragments, I took the opportunity to sort the stones based on their location within the gravesite, size, shape, and colour," Rhetta curtly detailed, as she walked towards the first three make-shift tables. "If you'd like to start reassembling them, I'll move onto examining the bone fragments."

"As you wish," Peter whispered, glad at being so trusted.

Based on Rhetta's preliminary findings the graveyard looked to have contained only eight singular plots - and just by noticing the various name fragments within the broken stones while sorting them, none of the deceased individuals shared similar surnames. Unlike most normal rural cemeteries, where there are plenty of interrelated Lockrows, Goyers, or Boomhowers - this surprised her. Even more surprising, there were no children's graves - which one would also presume to find in such a small country plot. She had expected this to be an extended family at least and not a gathering of strangers.

The first stone was simply broken in half. "This might be an easy fix," Peter thought. When he slid the two pieces together, he found that the monument belonged to Derek Hudson - a fellow who had died in 1954 at 67 years of age.

Now, I recall telling Peter many times to *think* things will be easy, but never ever to say so *out loud*. I'm not sure why, but the fates, or karma, or whatever, will take your self-assured pronouncement to heart and thwart your *should be easy* with an often confounding and mind-numbing *damnable difficult time*. Once, I spent four hours trying to fish an electrical wire through a horse-hair plaster wall that only had to go four feet down - after I loudly proclaimed that it would only take me ten minutes to complete. Lesson learned.

Once he had the base of the stone thoroughly fastened to the work table, the next thing Peter's Santa Fe pal had told him was to carefully wire brush all of the broken edges, just to get rid of all of the loose debris. At no time though, was he ever to use the wire brush on the face of the stone, as that might remove pertinent elements of historic data. Then, he was to check and see how well the pieces fit together and if there were any pieces missing. Mr. Hudson's stone fit very well together with no noticeable missing chunks, so Peter began mixing the two-part epoxy that would securely glue them together. The can's instructions required that he should use two-parts resin to one-part hardener, so that's what our dutiful Peter did.

In order to make the fix as invisible as possible, the grey-coloured polymer concrete had to be blended with pigment. His pal had suggested that he start by adding the black colorant first, and then move onto the white. In this instance, Peter was glad that he'd honed such a necessary skill through his years of painting. Despite my well-meaning and no doubt annoying instructional interferences, the boy could match any colour that he found in nature with perfect precision. Another Santa Fe suggestion was to mix in tiny broken fragments from the stone itself into the epoxy for a more ideal match.

With a firm brush, Peter pushed the epoxy mix deep into the grain on the corresponding sides of the broken pieces. Then, after he matched up the top and bottom portions of the stone, Peter aggressively pushed down setting the pieces firmly together. Quickly, he used a putty knife to trim away any excess cement that may have suddenly squirted out from between the joint.

"There," Peter announced with pride. "Derek Hudson's stone *is* done."

"That was pretty quick," Rhetta replied as she pushed a collection of matching-coloured finger bones into a pile. She'd already identified the eight pelvises.

"While this dries," Peter offered, "I'm going to see what I can find out about our Mr. Hudson via the internet."

"It's nice that Miss Lorraine had the cable company run a new line out here just for us to use."

"She's the best. Especially when she wants something good to happen."

"Well, we also know that Jefferson Wait is in here somewhere... ."

"Cool. That makes two identifications - Hudson and Wait."

"Yeah, now all I have to do is sort out and assemble these sixteen hundred bones - give or take a few that we might have left behind at the dig."

Note: a full grown human body has 206 bones in it - from a nearly 19" long pair of femurs to a collection of very minuscule cochlear ossicle bones in the inner ear. Now multiply that by eight and you've got a big job ahead of you.

Rhetta's work would be much more daunting and far more exacting than Peter's. While she too had to fit various pieces together like a jigsaw puzzle, there were also the questions as to gender, age, and whose skeleton belonged to who to be answered. Based on her preliminary findings - mostly based on pelvis shapes alone, as she hadn't yet assembled anything - there were probably three adult men, one juvenile male, and four adult females buried together.

"Women, you see," Rhetta had explained to Peter, "have a much wider pubic arch and a much shorter and pushed back sacrum. When he looked confused, she happily added, "you know, that large, triangular bone at the base of your spine. I could also use skull shape and size as a key determining factor. Women have rounder chins, while men's are more often square."

You may be surprised to learn that men's heads are both bigger and THICKER than a woman's. But you probably already knew that all along, now didn't you?

First she would have to painstakingly clean the remains and document everything that they told her. Unlike any traditional gravesite where the coffined remains are usually laid out in order from head to toe, the immoral developer's debris pile was a human salad with bits and pieces of the eight distinct souls sadly sprinkled like croutons all over the place.

As to age, had they all been children, Rhetta could've used whether they still had their deciduous (baby) or partial sets of primary teeth. If there were no teeth, she would have to determine which growth plates had sealed. The tibia plate, for example, usually seals around a child's middle or late teens. Earlier for girls and later for boys. The clavicle (the last bone in the body to complete its inevitable growth) generally seals itself around age 25. In adults, where there is little skeletal change - once all the plates have sealed - a whole different track of study is required. The use of arthritis levels - by determining the degree of rounding about the critical bones such as knees and elbows - could be one path. Arthritis and the number of osteons (*the fundamental functional unit of compact bone*) in the marrow, she knew, can also narrow down the potential age range for any skeleton.

Rhetta wouldn't know until after all the stones had been reassembled by Peter that determining the age of the skeletons really wouldn't be so important. All eight had been contemporaries - being born and later dying within ten years of one another.

As to identifying individuals, she would have to consider past fractures, which would be evident in any bone remodeling and might even explain the individual's cause of death. A fractured rib might indicate a collapsed lung or a misaligned spine - a broken neck. Wear and tear on bones via their muscle use, could indicate a hard working woman over that of an estate owner - who hired folks to do the work.

Post-mortem changes caused by soil, water, and any intrusions by plants, insects or other animals would also be considered as well.

Once she had a good idea, based on colour and visible age, of which fragments might belong together, Rhetta would then have to determine the quantity or extent of any available DNA found in each piece before she could extract it. Once the samples were given to the lab for polymerase chain reaction processing (where the DNA is copied, amplified, and its physical locations tagged) it might take two months before they received any results.

"Maybe after the DNA results are in we'll know if any of these folks are related."

"I can't wait," Peter replied excitedly. "It's a wonderful mystery!"

"We're not in any kind of hurry," she admonished him - again. "Remember what I said about this being a very pain-staking process."

"There's a terrible lot of work here though," Peter replied, looking a bit overwhelmed. "Hudson's was only the first stone of eight. This next pile might belong to some guy named Chris or some gal named Chris. The stone's been broken up into quarters, and I only have the first five letters of the first name and the birth year 1888 to go on so far."

"Patience my friend," Rhetta knowingly counseled. "We're not in a race. That person may've been dead for a hundred and fifteen years already.

Taking a few days to piece his or her stone back together won't change that."

"But we artists are an impatient lot," Peter joked. "Some of us need immediate gratification. That's why my Santa Fe pal is a serigrapher."

"It's the slow go that gives the greatest gratification," she offered suggestively. To which Peter heartily nodded in agreement.

When Peter looked up Derek Hudson on the internet, he found three possible entries for the time period that the fellow in question had lived. One was a farmer from Lewisville, Idaho, who was born in 1871. Another was an unlucky Canadian soldier who'd perished on November 11, 1918 - the very day that the first World War had ended. The last and most intriguing Derek Hudson was a cultured fellow who had graduated from the prestigious Académie Colarossi - an art school in Paris, France.

Artist Derek was indeed born French in the correct year etched on the stone of 1888. It also helped the investigation that he'd chosen to move to New York City when he was twenty-two to work primarily as a scene-painter in several off-Broadway theaters. Unlike the Idaho or Canadian Dereks, this propitious westward journey at least put him in the right quadrant to be eventually buried in upstate New York. Hudson remained at his craft, eventually becoming the principal set designer for the Greenwich Village based Stapleton Theater Company. When Pablo Picasso spent eight weeks in New York during the summer of 1924 (to produce designs for the company's production of the Dadaist play *The Gas-Operated Heart*) he worked in Hudson's studio on Bedford Street. During the Second World War, Hudson was mustered out after an explosion deformed his right hand. Even with his disability, during his rehabilitation, the artist managed to complete a small number of unnoticed Impressionistic landscapes - in the elegant style of George Inness. After his savings ran out, Hudson returned to scenery and set design. A small footnote regarding a serious bout with tuberculosis in his late sixties that sent the artist to, of all places, the Trudeau Sanitarium in Saranac Lake - only ninety miles from Lorraine's old property - cinched the deal. Not to mention that the old fellow died in the required year of 1954 - the same year that sanitarium closed.

"Did you by any chance find a mangled right hand amongst the skeletons?" Peter asked, as he walked over to Rhetta's work table. She was so lost in thought that she hadn't heard him approaching. He stole that brief moment to look at her - all beautiful in her sunlit repose.

"Actually, I did," she replied coming to life.

"That's going to be my number one - Mr. Derek Hudson Esquire. The man's right hand was severely damaged during the war."

"Here he is right here," Rhetta replied, looking quite happy. "Having you around is proving very useful... ."

"I've got other qualities too. You should see me dance... ."

"Sorry Peter," Rhetta joked. "As an expert in both anatomy and physiology, I can see your two left feet from here. Nope. There's not a dancin' bone in your whole body."

"Brilliant," Peter laughed. "Nice joke at my expense."

"I just relay 'em like I see 'em."

"So, while I'm bustin' my ass, workin' hard over there, you've been loafing here watchin' me?"

"Just close enough to make sure you're not gettin' yourself into any trouble."

"I suppose that's fair," Peter replied. "And as a forever student of aesthetics, I must admit, that I've also thoroughly observed you in your natural habitat."

"And what did you discover?" she asked almost demurely.

"That," he began sheepishly. "as a card-carryin' and oft-time employed artist, I fully appreciate your perfect physical form." When she gave him that bittersweet look of annoyed acceptance, he added, "too bad I can't see your exquisite brain. I'm sure that's amazingly beautiful too."

After Peter was able to reassemble the four broken sections of the second stone he learned that it belonged to a woman named Christabel Gilman - a contemporary of Derek Hudson. There were only two woman with that name found in his initial web-search. The fact that Christabel might have married or even remarried many times put a certain limit on his research - as each new surname widened the boundaries of the search criteria exponentially. The first woman was a well-known suffragette born in Manchester, Vermont in the correct year. "That's pretty close," Peter thought. "But why would she turn up buried outside Speculator?"

Then, when he came across Christabel number two and learned that the woman had been born in - of all places - Wells, formally known as Gilmantown, Peter knew he had his woman.

"Wells is just over the ridge from Lorraine's old property," he reasoned happily. "Still, what would bring her to be buried even that far from the sunny shores of Charley Lake?"

The following facts I know first-hand from having chatted with old Joshua Wells himself. He's the land agent that they named the town of Wells after. I suppose they wanted to thank him properly for having had the foresight to build those first few successful mills along Charley Lake. You know, the ones that brought so much needed prosperity to that once impecunious part of Hamilton County. He told me, as we both looked longingly out over that same placid lake

- as we dead folks love to do - that despite many valid attempts to reincorporate around 1860, the town of Gilman was eventually absorbed into Wells, NY. By the time Christabel arrived, nearly thirty years later, only the elderly folks in town remembered or ever used the old town's name. Josh (we're on a first name basis) told me that Christabel was the third child of the notorious Finch family and took the name Gilman as a way of separating herself from their murderous history. I think those are the folks that the lyrics *gave her mother forty whacks* came from - no, wait, that was Christabel's contemporary Lizzie Borden?

At any rate, Christabel changed her name for good reason, and went on to capture great images through the lens of her big glass-plate box camera - which was given to her as a gift by a wealthy uncle. Her soft focus style and treatment of photography as an art form - which is highly praised now - weren't so widely appreciated during the mid 1930's. Critics then called her work a collection of "frowzy mistakes" or, lacking in any verbal creativity themselves, simply bad photography. To my way of thinking, her body of work was more reminiscent in style to that of the European Pre-Raphaelites painters than to any of her black and white collodion contemporaries.

The seven-member Pre-Raphaelite Brotherhood, and I don't mean to be lecturing again, was founded in 1848, and wanted to reform art by returning to the lavish details, fierce colours, and elaborate compositions of 15th-century Italian art... and, given the same opportunity, who wouldn't?

Christabel's soft sepia-coloured images are all relevant portraits of common people - not celebrities or wealthy merchants and businessmen. They have value in that they tell as singular a story as any photo-journalist snapping world events. It has always been my feeling that had any artist of Ms. Gilman's undiscovered talent been supported by some wealthy and influential patron, who might capriciously decide to label her as avant guard or the next big thing, her life would have been much different. It might have been like mine, where I was embraced by an evocative wind that blew the sweet fragrance of acceptance my way. In this policy of random promotion, it's not always the will of the people, but the will of the one. Take fashion for example, when women's hemlines go up and down with the various seasons - only because one influential patron says that they should now be above the knee and the sheep follow, all while the money flows.

The third stone belonged to Reinhard Cecil Ryndes and its wonderful gaelic pattern made it fairly easy for Peter to reassemble. The gnarled strands and deeply etched celtic chains called out to each other - wanting sorely to be reunited. His research offered only three possible alternatives for the years indicated on the stone's face. A routinely unsuccessful politician from Salisbury, Massachusetts, a used car salesman from Dubuque, Iowa, (you'll agree that there really isn't much difference between these two gentlemen), and, are you seeing a trend evolving, a metaphorical painter from Succasunna, New Jersey.

Ryndes, born in 1886, was inspired by the classical antiquity of ancient Greece and Rome and specialized in figurative paintings involving landscapes with luxuriant gilded backgrounds. His painting of a very well proportioned woman pouring an urn full of warm water over her bare left shoulder while bathing is my personal favorite. Thankfully, Reinhard's earliest paintings were completed in watercolour, which served him well, for he often worked as an illustrator of books to make ends meet. Like his other two grave-mates, he never got inducted into the pantheon of the acclaimed. How R.C. Ryndes got buried in upstate New York was yet to be determined, but the fact that all three of the first stones belonged to struggling artists certainly must mean something.

The fourth stone had the name Cicely Ruth Norton and the dates 1895–1973 deeply inscribed upon its face. It was shattered into thirds, and took much time and patience for Peter to reassemble.

"Cicely Norton was an illustrator," Peter began, reading aloud, "modestly known too for her work on a series of children's books." Because of his perky earnestness, Rhetta thought he looked like a school boy standing there in short pants reading a theme. "Her education in art began with some correspondence courses and grew into full-time instruction at the The Grand Central School of Art - where she was among the first students ever to attend."

Being accepted by the Grand Central School of Art was no small matter. Founded in 1923 by the painters Edmund Greaten, Walter Leighten Clark and one of my personal favorite painters - John Singer Sargent, it was a formidable place. For twenty years the school occupied 7,000 square feet of the Grand Central Terminal's seventh floor. Cicely's fellow alumni include: Saturday Evening Post's Norman Rockwell, Canadian children's book illustrator Clare Bice, and Abstract expressionist Willem de Kooning.

Rhetta liked the tone of Peter's voice. It was strong, authoritative without any condescension, and most importantly, honest. She'd know men all her life who were either part carnival barker, part broadway showman, or life-long dedicated practitioners of deceit - where the first lie was always free.

"Her earliest professional work," Peter continued, unaware of Rhetta's gentle inspection, "included designing greeting cards and even some accepted submissions to *The Dayspring* and *Child Lore* juvenile magazines."

Peter's pleasant baritone rang with searing fidelity, fierce loyalty, and sheer unsullied credibility. She was happily realizing that he was like no man she'd ever met before.

"Norton's first book *"Fairy Spring"* was published in 1943," he continued. "Similar works for both summer and autumn were also published over the next three decades. Unfortunately, they never really gained much critical attention."

What was preventing Rhetta from allowing Peter's gentle pursuit of her? I'm guessing that she was weary of getting hurt - again. Most of the men that she'd encountered before him weren't ever going to allow her as an equal partner, wanting mostly to control and overshadow her. Concealing herself within the cloak of her work had become her norm, and allowing that curtain to fall would be hard for her.

The fifth grave marker belonged to the oldest man so far - Sawrey Cockerell, who had been born in the midst of the American Civil War and died 88 years later during an equally hate-filled era - Joe McCarthy's 1950's Red Scare. Having the same last name as Rhetta gave her pause. Could Sawrey be a lost or distant relative?

The four most notable aspects of Sawrey's skeletal stature - once he'd been properly assembled - was that his height was just under four feet 10 inches, that his legs were rather bowed at the knees, that his back was slightly hunched, and that his strong jaw was fairly overcrowded with teeth.

"He was a dwarf and not a juvenile male like I first thought," Rhetta whispered to herself. "I'd have never seen it until all the bones were aligned." Then, with brightness, she added, "that should make it much simpler for Peter to determine which of our internet Sawrey Cockerell's is our man."

Sawrey, as a different, and for that period in history an embarrassing person, found himself relegated to the family's back porch in the summer and back bedroom in the winter. Unlike the fine china, Sawrey was never brought out when guests came to the house. He was never invited on walks or to go on family outings - like his much more normal-looking siblings. Left to his own devices and with a strong desire to be seen - if only for his work - Sawrey began creating art through the arrangement of scrap fabrics and found textiles. Experiments with watercolours finally led him to his passion when he started creating beautiful batik panels.

Batik is an ancient Chinese technique of wax-resist dyeing and is made by either using a spouted tool called a *canting* or by painting the wax with a brush onto cloth. The applied wax resists water-based dyes and allows the artist to colour selectively by immersing the fabric in one colour, removing the wax with boiling water, and repeating the process depending on how many colours are required for the composition. It's like serigraphy, only different.

When Rhetta contacted her mother to ask about any possible family connection with Sawrey, she was surprised by her answer. The little man who was born in 1863, was indeed a distant relative. It may have been six generations into the past, but Sawrey was her father's long lost grand uncle. There had been little or no mention of him through the years, and absolutely no photographs. The only visible markers of his time spent on this planet were remnants of his colorful batiks. There were framed pieces that her mother knew about that were still being held in private collections, and even some faded scarfs made from his designs. When pressed, Rhetta's mother had no idea where her husband's uncle had been buried in 1951, only that he'd moved north when his mental acuity had begun to fail.

"You're back in the family Uncle," Rhetta whispered to Sawrey's earth-stained ocher skull, as she held it out like Shakespeare's poor Yorick. "You'll not be alone again. Not if I can help it."

You're probably asking yourself, why couldn't good ol'Gabriel just go poking through his vast array of etherial haunts and round up these eight particular specters and find out just who the hell is who? Why not settle this damn thing quick and easy? Well, that's not as simple a task as you might think, and even if I did mange to collect all that pertinent information, how the hell would I be able to let Rhetta and Peter know? It's not like they can hear me.

Up at the Moose Lake house, Saoirse's paramour was just about to return from Redden for a long weekend visit. His new teaching position at the

Wainwright Academy had begun with the fall semester. While he'd been busy in the south for the past two months instructing overly ernest pupils on the correct way to hold a brush or set up a proper colour pallet, she'd been plenty occupied writing her *Four Artists* oeuvre. Now that the initial research had been completed on each of their biographies, she'd start working out the various story arcs, hoping to find some common ground and possibly even a method of unifying them all into a single satisfying ending.

As time consuming as all that was, she'd also been quite busy on another monumental task. This one, while requiring far less outward effort - especially now that the morning vomiting had gratefully ended, seemed to be proceeding quite naturally on its own. When the first monthly cycle didn't show its familiar crimson ensign, she became a little concerned. Up until last September, her procreative works had been performing like clockwork - fabricating a fertile home for an egg and then flushing it all away when nothing took seed. When the second month's flag didn't unfurl as well, she was both elated and fearful. Joyful at the idea of having created life, just as her mother had. Frightful of the facts, that once known to the world, might colour her blameless child's future.

She had taken to wearing loose fitting sweaters so that her requisite bodily transformations mightn't be so noticeable to the general public. Although, given the Scotsman's keen eye for detail, there'd be no way of hiding the fact that she now possessed enormous boobs.

"He's used to a handful," she pondered as she looked casually down the neckline of her blouse the morning before his arrival. "Wait'll he gets a load of these babies."

"Hoo is mah wee lassie," Chord offered brightly, as he stepped through the door. "Ye sure loch like yoo've bin busy."

As usual, the mere sight of Chord Murtagh standing in your hallway was a joy to behold. It made your heart quicken, your breath come and go with an audible aww, and firmly escalated your desire to be held in his sinewy arms - and I'm only speakin' for myself. I can't image what a full-blooded woman like Saoirse was feeling at that very moment.

"It's grand to see you," she mumbled, still captured by his overwhelming handsomeness. "What took you so long getting here?"

"I hud tae wark," he lamely explained. "Th' college expects me tae put in a full week, dornt ye know!"

"I'm not talkin' about the last two months you idiot," she playfully corrected him. "I'm talkin' about today! Couldn't you have gotten up earlier and been here two hours ago?"

"Ah did gie up early, but thaur was a lot ay traffic?"

"Rent a helicopter next time... ."

"Och aye, Ah will," he replied, as he slowly shifted his gaze from her eyes." He, it turns out, enjoyed the sight of such a comely lass as well. "Gie us a hug 'en. Ah want tae wrap mah arms aroond ye."

"I couldn't imagine a better plan," she replied hesitantly. There was no way he wouldn't guess her secret after one of his full-bodied embraces. So before he was able to get any closer, she reluctantly added, "there's something that I need to share with you."

"Afair mah hug?"

"Yes. Before your hug," she replied, as she slowly pulled up her sweater and revealed her slightly plump belly. "Seems, you've gotten your wish."

"Mah wish... ?"

"Yeah. You remember. The day you came up here unannounced and made me fall in love with you all over again... ."

"Ah. That fine day... ."

"Well your wish to become a father may have come true."

"That was quick daein'," he replied with a quizzical look. "By th' looks ay ye, there's wee doobt concernin' yer condition." Then after a few moment's of puzzled consideration, he asked, "wa dae ye say mah dream may have come true?"

"I can't abide you ever lying to me," she said firmly, "so I won't ever do that to you. I will always tell you the truth - the absolute truth, no matter how much it hurts."

"Ah appreciate that... an' Ah vow th' sam."

"It embarrasses me to admit this," she began hesitantly. "And it only happened the one time... but

Peter and I made love a few nights before you showed up unannounced on my doorstep."

"Ye did whit wi' peter?" Chord wasn't exactly sure he'd heard her correctly.

"Made love... ."

His first reaction was anger - the violent kind, but that passed quickly after he caught the sincere look of need in her eyes. Saoirse clearly required that he understand how that singular event had happened and why.

"Christ! I thought you were already married to Claire... ."

Seeing the nearly instantaneous transformation from hateful misinterpretation to devoted understanding in his expression, allowed Saoirse to continue, "at that extremely low point in my miserable life, I needed someone to hold me, recognize my pain, and then, not hold on too tightly afterwards... ."

"Lovin' ye, an' lettin' go, how is that even possible?" Chord replied, before thinking it through. His face suddenly stiffened, as though he were struggling to unwind two divergent thoughts. "Ah," he finally admitted, "Ah did bonnie much th' sam thin' when Ah left ye fur Claire. Ah put ye in that miserable state ay life myself."

"It wasn't love, at least not on my part," Saoirse offered sincerely, as she tenderly touched Chord's arm. "As for Peter, I think it was more the fulfillment of an old dream. A teenage desire - really. Something that he needed to do, but honestly believed wouldn't last in the bright light of day. If you think about it, Peter was doing me a kindness, so don't be cross with him."

"So, Aam thinkin'," he offered sadly, after some additional consideration, "that Aam th' a body tae blame. If Ah hadnae bin such a drunken coward an' left ye, yoo'd have ne'er been put in such a disastroos yearnin'."

"That sounds like forgiveness... ."

"It's me that's askin' fur forgiveness... ."

Saoirse leaned in and kissed Chord dearly and his returning it with the same fervor, succinctly signaled their arrival at a mutual absolution.

"What if little Rose Lyric isn't yours?" Saoirse ventured once the dust had settled a bit. "It's a few months too early to know for sure, but I'm fairly certain it'll be a girl."

"So, yoo've named 'er efter mah mamm... ."

"Was that wrong?"

"Nae. Rose woods have loo'd havin' 'er granddaughter shaur 'er nam."

"What about Peter... ?"

"Hae ye tauld heem?"

"No. I wanted to tell you first. I'm not really sure how he'll respond... ."

"He's likely tae go yer way oan this.... He diz loove ye."

"What about you though? Are you Ok with all this?"

Doing the unemotional math, Chord quickly considered that if providence did go his way, little Rose would be at least 50% his, and if it didn't, she'd still be

100% Saoirse's - and that would be more than good enough.

"How's heem bein' Rose's Godfaither - suit ye.?

"It suits me fine," she replied, happy that the Scotsman had surely matured since their breakup. "Just so long as you don't mind that Peter's a practicing agnostic."

Now, I recall telling you about Saoirse's first husband Richard and his inability to succor an innocent child that was not his own - resulting in that poor child's death. It was a complete lack of character I said. To his credit, it wasn't the same with Chord when he had to face the same challenge. For over six hundred years, from the time of William Wallace and Robert the Bruce, the men of the Murtagh family had always held the high ground in both temperament and character. The fact that he would choose to give up dear Saoirse's love rather than chance his hurting their yet to be conceived child - because of his own deficiencies due to alcohol - spoke clearly to that historic character. His ability to rise above any petty jealousies regarding her time spent with another man - especially during her period of incredible depression, and recognizing that it was by his very own actions that'd put her in that desperate place, sings proudly of that heraldic quality as well. By this gesture alone, he is every bit the hero she met on that NYC subway platform that evening before going to the Empire State Building. By my judgement, he is a fine man and quite worthy of my dear niece's affection.

"There's going to be a wedding!" Rhetta shouted. "Chord's asked Saoirse to marry him!"

"That should make Saoirse very happy," Peter replied, a little flattened by the bittersweet news. "She's been wantin' that to happen for some time now."

In his heart-of-hearts Peter knew Saoirse's love for the Scotsman was true, and that this was a very good thing, but his feelings for her would always be both tender and protectively solicitous - especially now that she was with child.

Since his adolescence, he'd dreamed of protecting her - being her white knight so-to-speak. A childhood fantasy made real by his actually having been able to make love to her was well beyond his wildest imaginings. Even an angel, he now realized, could become real in the heated throws of human passion. That sweet catalyst ignited an overwhelming metamorphosis - finally setting him free from her unwitting and yet captivating spell. Now, as he looked over at Rhetta, so uncharacteristically excited by this wedding news, he began to feel differently. Chord would always protect Saoirse and her child - with his life if need be. Who would protect Rhetta? Surely, she was capable of defending herself, but who would look out for her? Be there for her? Comfort her? Love her?

He would.

Now, if I had anything to say about it, I'd have told Peter with the same insistence for absolute truth as Saoirse had chosen to provide Chord, that little Rose might be his child as well. Recognizing the timing, and lack of protection, Peter suspected as much without having to be told, but chose not to pursue the issue - given that Saoirse would always be in his life, so whether he fathered the child formally or less so, he'd still have love in his heart for both mother and child.

"Saoirse is keeping her name," Rhetta continued. "I plan on doing the same, should ever I decide to marry."

"Wait," Peter said, as he paused to pick up his note book. "That's the missing link. Stones number six and seven are married, but they each kept their own names and, for some reason, had separate stones made."

"That doesn't sound very logical to me," Rhetta replied, reluctantly returning to her work. Part of her was still quite giddy over Saoirse's news. "Keeping my own name wouldn't prevent me from wanting to be buried with my husband."

"Yeah. But what if the second stone was needed because one of the bodies was buried elsewhere and then moved to our graveyard?"

"That's certainly possible... ."

"At least we'd have found *one* strong connection between two of these eight disparate souls."

"Yeah, Something more than their all being artists."

Peter's research on the final two skeletons revealed that Gates Fennel Rollins met her much younger Macedonian paramour Faina Kostadin in 1902, while both were in residence at the Museum of Fine Arts in Boston. Gates, quite gifted with the use of pastels, was acting as the museum's paintings curator at that time and Faina was a newly enrolled sculpture student in the Francis Davis Millet's Art School - which had a long affiliation with the museum.

They met in front of Fine Arts Museum one delightful summer afternoon, after each of them had decided to take a stroll alone through Copley Square. They'd seen each other a few times before, across rooms and on staircases, but had never been properly introduced. By the time they reached Trinity Church they were walking arm-in-arm together, quickly recognizing their deep attraction for one another. Frequent meetings were planned and pleasantly executed, and after returning from a lovely streetcar ride to visit the shores of the Charles River, the women found themselves enjoying the intimate delights of a sunlit room in the Hotel Westminster. At the turn of the century, their perfect love could not yet see the light of day, but undaunted and without the need for heralding trumpets, their hearts held fast to their mutual affections.

When Peter came across the random fact that both women had visited the Siwa Oasis in Egypt in 1914, he decided to research the place. It is literally an oasis set mid-way between the Qattara Depression and the megaduned Sand Sea, some 350 miles west of Cairo and just thirty miles east of the Libyan border. He found that this splendid western desert oasis had had a historical acceptance of homosexuality even as far back as 1900 and actually allowed rituals for performing binding same-sex marriages.

"The girls went to where the world would openly accept their love," Peter whispered, allowing the words to hold greater solemnity with sound. "Maybe there's a marriage license floating around some place?"

Of course there wasn't. There never *is* when you really really want there to be. But dutiful Peter persevered. In a random search for both women's names at the same time, a property deed - smudged badly through too many xeroxes - suddenly appeared on-line. It was dated 1947, just two years before Gates had died at the age of 89. The ladies in love, it turned out, had once owned a small plot of land just outside Wells, NY.

"I was right about six and seven, or should I say Gates and Faina," Peter told Rhetta when she returned to the garage. "They were married and the fact that they were lesbian lovers explains why they couldn't share a stone... ."

"Or each other's last name," Rhetta replied.

"Sad isn't it," Peter offered, with a downcast look, "that some folks just can't see love is love - no matter who you feel it for. A person can't help the way they are innately wired."

"You love who you love," Rhetta knowingly agreed. "I get that. Why can't other folks see something so natural?"

"Because, I 'spect," Peter offered, still looking forlorn, "they've gotta run everybody else's life as well as there own. *My way or the highway,* my old man used to say."

"Tell me about it," Rhetta vented. "Just try growing up black in America. There are folks all over the damn country looking to put me in my place. First because I'm a woman, but mostly just because of the colour of my skin."

"It's a beautiful shade of mahogany," Peter whispered to himself.

"Growing up in Ellwood Park in Baltimore taught me how to fend for myself. I don't let anyone push me around - not since I was three years old. If I loved a woman, she'd be mine, and I'd shout it to the world - not giving a single care as to who could hear me!"

"You don't though - right? Love a woman?"

"No Peter," Rhetta answered, enjoying the look of sudden dismay in his eyes. "I was just making a point."

"Gotcha," Peter mumbled, sorry that what he'd meant to keep safely silent in his brain had somehow managed to seep out.

The mostly black middle-class neighborhood where Rhetta grew up did include a small public park. Ellwood Park was that virescent place over between Jefferson and Orleans Streets, with a tiny playground and occasional sunshine. Most folks, including Rhetta's family lived in two-story red-brick row houses. The coloured awnings and painted porch roofs sometimes kept out the grey, but Baltimore grey is most insidious. It sticks to your memories and can't easily be shaken off. Because of her budding love of science, you'd most likely find our girl alone on the family's front porch quietly examining the bones of some dead bird or other hapless critter that she'd found. Like any child with a machine, she just had to find out how our bodies worked. Those five red-brick front steps made an excellent work table for her to explore her world - bone by bone.

"This skeleton definitely belongs to Mr. Wait," Rhetta announced to Peter, quite certain of her findings. "You see the nasal aperture here," she continued, pointing to Wait's skull with the end of her pencil, "it's more flared and shorter than any of the other males we found, plus it has a lower bridge with a guttered nasal sill." Then rolling the skull around and pointing to just above where the neck bone should be, she added, "plus, his mastoid process is far wider than any of the others. The three other male's all have narrow and pointed bone projections here, suggesting that they are white. And, as if any more proof were necessary, the left and right maxillary bones that form the roof of Wait's mouth are hyperbolic - classical African architecture."

"So," Peter began, "we now know who three of the skeletons belong to? There's Mr. Wait - who you've just identified. Mr. Hudson with the mangled right hand and Mr Cockerel - the person of short stature."

"Four, or maybe even five," Rhetta corrected. "Based on the calcium deposits and the implied muscle development, I'm surmising that number seven is Faina Kostadin... ."

"Because she was the sculptor who worked with marble... ."

"Yes, having to maneuver all those heavy blocks would be a valid contributing factor for her having such enlarged bones."

"And the fifth conclusion... ?"

"There was a silver wedding ring embedded around one of the female's fingers - with the name Finch inscribed on it."

"Why, Finch was the name that Christabel Gilman was born with... ."

"Exactly."

"That leaves just Reinhard Ryndes, Cicely Norton, and Gates Rollins... ."

"Well, yes and no," Rhetta replied with a smile. "If we know who Hudson, Wait, and Cockerel are, by process of elimination, that leaves only one unclaimed male skeleton for Mr. Ryndes to be assigned to."

"Great!," Peter replied happily. "Now all we have to do is sort out Ms. Cicely and Ms. Norton."

"I'd rate them by age, but according to their headstones, they're too close to differentiate properly, what with one being 78 and the other 89," Rhetta said. not sounding a bit annoyed. "Anything over sixty years doesn't test reliably."

"How about some dental records? Maybe we could find some of those?"

"That would work wonderfully well.... . Got any?"

"Maybe," Peter replied, sounding rather quizzical. "I'm thinkin' that if Gates and Faina lived locally, there just might be some medical records left on file for them over in Wells."

"It's certainly worth a telephone call... ."

"Or maybe a ride? We could step out for a change and get some dinner?"

"Fine. Can we find a place that has key lime pie? I'd simply love some key lime pie."

"Pickin's are pretty slim around here what with gettin' any kind of pie," Peter offered with a grin, "but let's chance it. Maybe the Wren's Nest Inn over near Pleasant Lake is still around?"

"Does that place belong to someone you know?"

"No. Not really. It's under new ownership now. Atwell used to take me there when I was a kid because he knew the chef's grandfather, and we'd get our eats for free."

"Well, it's your invitation, so my eats *are* free," Rhetta replied with a laugh.

"OK," Peter agreed, happily seeing the joke. "A date it is."

"Date?" Rhetta questioned.

"If I'm payin' for your eatin' then it's a date."

"Really," she replied with very little real concern for his using the term.

"I just relay 'em like I see 'em." Peter offered mimicking her from before, which she also didn't seem to mind.

There's nothing like the smell of an Adirondack afternoon - especially after a subtle rain has just fallen. It makes the highway's surface a crisp reflective sable full of shadows and allows the random staccato of puddle splashes to sound with each tire roll. Then, as the tantalizing aroma of fresh pine and wildflowers washes over your senses, all seems right with the world again. At least until you come up behind your first Oshkosh M911 tractor trailer hauling a full load of logs.

"The mountains are full of trees," a tune from one of Lorraine's beginner piano books had read, *"which draws the lumbermen like fleas, and requires the big rigs to haul it all down ... to build all the pretty cities."*

Having a diesel Oshkosh chugging along in front of you, even spewing plumes of diesel fumes, is a good thing sometimes - especially if you wanted to be alone for a spell with the young woman of your dreams.

"You never ever talk about your havin' a boy friend," Peter ventured after a prolonged dry spell in the conversation. Small talk really wasn't one of Rhetta's favorite pastimes. *How's the weather - fine,* and that was about all that she'd allow.

"That's because there's nothing to say on that subject," Rhetta replied offhandedly, choosing to look away from him and out the window. A high wide wall of grey igneous rock that was being randomly dissected by tiny waterfalls had caught her eye.

"But you're so beautiful," he wanted to say, and something about *moths to a flame,* but chose to stifle the words.

"I've never really had much time for frivolous passions," she finally admitted, still not looking at him. "Getting an education was my sole focal point, mostly because it would get me out of Baltimore."

"Yeah, and you've done that well enough," Peter replied, saddened by her commitment to only enhancing half her world. "Now that you've attained such professional success, you really ought to take yourself on a nice fatuous vacation from it all."

"And that would be under your experienced guidance?"

"Are you calling me or my work silly?"

"Aren't they the same thing when it comes to you being an artist?"

Rhetta does have a point there. Almost all of the artist-types that I ever knew personally were either irreverent, rash, or simply foolhardy personalities. Except for maybe Marc Chagall, a modernist, who spent his war years in Soviet Belarus, where everything is much too somber. It seriously ruined his ability to be silly.

"I'm guessing that work for you is a passion," Peter began. "And you'll allow that mine is for me as well?"

"Certainly... Are you *ever* going to pass this damn truck?"

"On this winding mountain road!? Are you crazy!?"

"Nope. Just hungry."

"Maybe the trucker will be pullin' off soon...?"

"That's what I'm saying silly head," Rhetta replied with a mordant smile, "your sheer optimism that that may actually happen is wonderfully foolhardy, especially when all the evidence to date indicates that there hasn't been any intersecting side roads for it to turn off on for the last ten miles or more."

"What's wrong with a little optimism?"

"Nothing. Just so long as you don't let it get the better of you."

"You had to be fairly optimistic when you agreed so quickly to help Saoirse with all the sortin' and identifyin' in her little tossed graveyard?"

"I'd call it confidence," Rhetta replied self-assuredly. "Trust that the natural facts of the various cases would eventually reveal themselves... ."

"So, for you, science is just facts?"

"*Science is the knowledge of consequences*," she replied quoting English philosopher Thomas Hobbes, "*and dependence of one fact upon another.*"

"And without passion?" Peter wondered.

"I do have passion, but only for the process," Rhetta argued. "I could never allow my emotions to invade and cloud my critical thinking. I must leave the truth to speak of its own accord."

"I know that it's far less critical," Peter replied, "but, in my work, I must speak the truth as well. My canvas must articulate not only with emotion but with the sheer integrity of the existing view. Otherwise, it's all false conjecture and not worth payin' any attention to."

"Are art and science so really different then?" Rhetta wondered, softening her position. "They both require righteous fervor as well as sterling intellect to make them worthy of our time and energy."

"At first, I thought you preferred the lonely scholarly exploration of facts and findings, but without someone like Saoirse to relish in those discoveries, you'd be just like me, if no one ever saw one of my finished canvas."

"Every scientific truth goes through three distinct states," Louis Agassiz, a spectral biologist that I recently met floating around Cambridge, Mass, once said. *"First, people say it conflicts with the bible; next, they say it has been discovered before; lastly, they say that they have always believed it."*

Well, I know that I've always believed it and I'm not surprised that its taken so much time for the kids to see that truth for themselves. They were so busy in their spirited debate that neither of them saw the gigantic eighteen-wheeler pull off onto a logging road. When the road dust cleared and the truck's giant shadow disappeared, the afternoon sun gladly returned, this time illuminating not only their animated faces, but a budding sense of their mutual desire.

"The Wren's Nest is just up ahead," Peter declared. The look of sudden satisfaction on Rhetta's face told him either that she'd thought she won their argument or that she'd finally get a meal after an hour's ride. He wasn't sure either way.

Their table was set mid-room, right in front of a stone fireplace. With her back to the leaded-windows, the sun cast a soft apricot halo about Rhetta's head - as if she could look any more angelic to our dutiful Peter.

The waitress came and handed each of them a menu. Then, taking a rigid stance, with her heels firmly touching, she recited a very well practiced litany of the daily specials. When she finished, she nodded and then walked briskly away - leaving them free to consider their many choices.

Before they could order, Rhetta excused herself, leaving Peter alone to occupy himself for a few moments. His chilled glass of water certainly tasted mountain-fresh, but drinking it only took up a few seconds. Turning to the menu, he passed by all of the fine offerings, choosing to examine the back page - where some restaurants include a bit of local folklore to help pass the time. The Wren's Nest Inn, it turns out, was quite proud to share its expansive Adirondack history with its mostly transient clientele, knowing that basting with antiquity was just as helpful to the flavor as any other seasoning. As Peter poured over the information, he was taken by one particular item - the original owner of the Inn was listed as Reinhard C. Ryndes. Could that be the man his father used to know? Could that also be the same fellow that had been buried in Saoirse's disheveled cemetery?

You'll remember that Ryndes was born in 1886 and specialized in figurative paintings involving vast landscapes with luxuriant gilded backgrounds. Well, the Wren's Nest Inn was full of them. Peter had been so taken with being alone with Rhetta, that he hadn't noticed any of the paintings until just now.

Above the fireplace was a wide canvas showing a red-caped man (looking a bit like Sir Issac Newton) holding an apple alongside a burbling river. His sanguined contemplation was not at all disturbed by the murder of angels floating unnoticed all around him. Upon closer inspection, Peter could see the artist's signature: R.C. Ryndes and the date of 1948. The duel portrait on the wall to his left above the Victorian settee showed an angelic knight also seated by a river, with a young saffron clad damsel closely observing him. The armored fellow is too busy reading his precious psalms to notice the young woman's heaving bosom. This painting and three others were also all signed by Ryndes.

"It's him," Peter mumbled to himself. "It's gotta be!"

"What's all the excitement?" Rhetta wanted to know when she returned to their table.

"It's R.C. Ryndes, that's who!"

"Skeleton number three?"

"Yep! He's the original owner of this Inn," Peter excitedly told her. "And all these paintings are his!"

"That explains the Inn's name," Rhetta speculated. "Wren's Nest sounds an awful lot like Ryndes, doesn't it?"

"At least the Ellis Island pronunciation," Peter countered, not exactly sure how the name was properly said.

"At any rate, all this certainly puts him firmly in the Adirondacks. Now all we have to do is figure out how he wound up buried in Lorraine & Saoirse's back yard?"

Dinner was ordered, and at Peter's suggestion, Rhetta decided to try the rainbow trout. Never having had a freshly-caught fish, she wanted to fully immerse herself in the Adirondack experience. Which, as the wine flowed, and the conversation got more and more personal, was beginning to include the possibility of making love to one of the handsome local lads - Peter.

Having Rhetta out in the world and also away from her work was a unique and pleasant experience. Peter always enjoyed her lively banter in the shop or out in the field, but now listening to her witty and informed conversation, he liked her even more. In her delightful presence, Peter often found that his heart palpitated, causing him to experience near breathlessness, which in turn robbed him of his general equilibrium. Like any other heady and intoxicating stimulus, being with Rhetta was becoming feverously addicting. He would definitely need more and larger doses.

Sitting there with Peter, generally relaxed and easily conversing, Rhetta found no awkward moments or periods of stale conversation. As she noted before, the man knew stuff and was quite capable of sharing his well informed opinions. Her first impression had been that he was just another pretty boy, like Saoirse's hunky Adonis Chord Murtagh, but she was wrong about both men. Upon closer inspection, each of them had proven that they were thoughtful and complicated people - certainly worthy of any woman of substance's time.

Truth be told, Peter really wasn't Rhetta's type - that is if she actually did have a type. Artists and musicians usually didn't grab her attention the way that the sterling men of science generally did. Maybe it was the padded-shoulders of their white lab coats or the fellows' big brains, I don't know. At any rate, she figured that poor Peter didn't know how to speak her language, at least not nearly as fluently as all the other men she'd chosen to make love to. That didn't mean he couldn't be taught that grander articulation, or on the other hand, that he might be worthy of her taking the time to study his precious lexicon of aesthetics. She was on the fence, but leaning, definitely leaning.

"You know Peter," Rhetta began, repeating what he'd started in the car, "in all the time that I've known you, you've never mentioned, much less gone out with any women."

"Really?" he replied, suddenly flipping madly through the scattered chapters of his memory. The last woman, before Saoirse, that he could recall being out with was Lisbeth Santoro, from the Laguna Gallery. "No. No, I haven't have I?"

"Don't you like girls?" Rhetta teased - for she already knew the answer. Like any worldly woman, she was fully aware of all his so-called hidden desires for her.

"I do. I do like girls very very much. Some even more than all the others."

"And who might that be?"

"I'll tell you after you finish your wine. Waiter! Another bottle of Malbec!"

"Someone might think that you're trying to get me drunk... ."

"No. Not at all. The wine is totally for medicinal purposes only."

"Medicinal, you say?"

"Totally!"

"You're going to have to explain that... and please use **big** words."

"OK, it's a little embarrassin' - and I only mention this because of strict health related concerns - but... my love making, by both consensus and definition," Peter joked, "can sometimes cause parts of a woman's body to become - well - flushed and sort of swollen - and in rare cases, inflamed. It's a gift really. Medically, you might even call me an *inflammation*."

When Rhetta's laughter finally ceased, the whole restaurant was looking at her - including their waiter, who, in the confusion, had dropped their new bottle of Malbec on the floor.

"Waiter!" Rhetta called out loudly, totally unconcerned about having suddenly acquired a rapt audience. "Bring me my medication!" Then as her array of confused gawkers slowly dissipated and the sound of clinking knives and forks returned, she added rather enticingly, "come on Mr. *Transportation*, how about you transport me upstairs and we try out one of the rooms?"

"What! No key lime pie!?" Peter asked kiddingly, for he could hardly wait to get her upstairs. "I was promised key lime pie!"

"Oh, there'll be dessert all right... it'll come along with the room service... ."

Yep... the two crazy kids went upstairs - but I didn't. So, I'm going to let your sweet imaginations fire alone on what may or may not have occurred up there. Let me remind you though, that both of them are experienced lovers and, coming from very different amorous disciplines, had much to teach one another. Where do you suppose *dutiful* Peter got his name? Based on the enduring commotion witnessed by their sleep-deprived neighbors in the adjoining rooms, their excited and impassioned disquisition lasted for much of the night.

As an aside here... sure, I could have certainly stayed and watched their whole provocative rumpus unfold, that is if you like viewing some awkward x-rated film where the stars are only people you personally know. Like most of you would, given similar parameters, I just chose not to. Now, take this thought one step further. You know when you're in the act of doing something you wouldn't ever want your loving Nana to witness - well, I'm telling you right now that if she's passed on, she can, and often does. So, for your own benefit... knock it off. Don't be a lying politician, don't steal that car just because the keys got left in the ignition, or beat your innocent wife just because you're a stupid tool - grandma **is** watching. She's not judging you, just taking careful notes for when she catches up with you on this side of the etherial plane and gives you hell!

Later, when Peter and Rhetta drove back to Moose Lake, they noticed that the road home was eminently smoother, and that the air was so much sweeter than they'd remembered it being the previous day. It didn't escape either one of them that they each saw the other in a softer light now - as if a future fertile plane had been successfully sown between them. That harsh light meant for observing and deflecting strangers would no longer be required between them.

Ah... the soft focus of love.

Soon, they would gladly stand up at a fine wedding, when a white-laced Saoirse and an olive-kilted Chord happily tied the knot. Dear Lorraine was there as well, standing in for me, to happily give the bride away. Unfortunately for most of the female spectators (and some of the attending fellows), due to current contemporary fashion morays, Chord's kilt was set well below his knees that day. Along with the spirited cheers, there were some doleful tears, mostly at my not being there to witness the joyous festivities, but that was only because those kind folks couldn't see me ethereally dancing my many merry jigs and repeatedly kissing the rosy cheeks of the winsome bride.

"Sláinte!"
"Your good health!"

PART SIX

When the eight headstones finally got replanted, they looked like a classroom full of kids after their teacher had asked who threw that damn eraser - all shrugs. Tucked in neat little rows of four over four, they were all of a similar design, except for the Celtic knots on R.C. Ryndes's marker which had come from across the sea. Now skirting the boneyard's perimeter was a vintage 1880's wrought iron fence that Saoirse located in Philadelphia. It consisted of a series of narrow vertical rods that at regular intervals arched over a single fleur-de-lis, like a hoop over an arrow. This rounded look was far less harsh than that of the more pointed standard cemetery rods and better suited to this particular style of headstone - at least according to Lorraine's keen aesthetic.

"A jaggedly fence just won't do," she declared at one planning meeting. "It's too violent looking for such an artful place."

Thanks to Rhetta's fine forensics, all of the remains had been named and reunited with their fellow fingers and fragments. "Ten fingers and ten toes," Peter heard her shout at least eight times, as each collection became complete. When the DNA results arrived, they matched perfectly with Rhetta's competent interpretation of the facts. At Saoirse's suggestion, Gates and Faina were allowed to share a single coffin.

"If not in life, then for all eternity," Saoirse whispered as the undertaker sealed their lid.

The whole tiny cemetery happened because those two women had desired a home together. The Adirondacks, they knew, could supply a private haven where they could quietly love each other openly and not be so vehemently scrutinized by an uneducated and seemingly heartless society. Of course, there would likely be hateful fanatics in the mountains too. Folks who were dead-sure that their interpretation of the bible wasn't pointed parables, but pure unadulterated fact. Thankfully, due to the general spareness of the Adirondack population, those folks were few and far between.

It would have been better if they were far enough apart as to not reproduce, so that their skewed point of view might simply die out on its own, but those folks always seem to find one another - and then they breed like rabbits.

The demolished house that Peter and Saoirse had found near the vista was Gates and Faina's - built by their own design - with six large bedrooms and a grand center salon. Their intention was to invite all of their ill or fading friends to join them there - a commune of dying artists as it were. Whether the fatal malady be via the floundering of unfound fame, the devastating pain of unrequited love, or simply escalating poor health - all were welcome. That's why the names on the gravestones didn't match as they might have been expected to with a buried extended family. Although, one could argue that despite the varied names, these folks were indeed a family in both kind and deed.

When no one was looking, I put out a siren's call to see if I could round up these eight fragile souls for a bit of a sit down regarding what life was like in their old communal homestead. It was literally a shot-in-the-dark, for communications on this side of reality are pretty spotty at best. It turns out, you'll be happy to hear, that none of the big media conglomerates can successfully transcend the fragile span of any such epoch with their guileless radio transmissions. Bullshit just doesn't grow wings over here. The real truth is that most of my fellow spirits are too busy listening to the sounds of nature for the first time and can no longer tolerate the grating choir of harsh or shrill human voices. That's one of the reasons why we etherials get caught up watching pooling or rushing water wherever we can find it. The burbles and the bubbles and the ripples for some reason bring us peace.

Just as before, when Lorraine found those four paintings, the first phantasm to show was Jefferson Wait. He was everything that I imagined - tall, hardy looking - even for the departed - and inquisitive as anything.

"Have you been wanderin' long?" Jefferson wanted to know right off, not even waiting for an introduction.

"No," I replied. "Not nearly as long as you."

"I only ask 'cause I want to share in what you've seen and done since crossin' over... you know... add your consciousness to mine... ."

"I've not done nearly so much while wanderin' as you," I respectfully replied. "You're journey's been nigh unto fifty years now, while mine's been but its mere fraction... ."

"Fifty you say? It seems like but a sneeze to me... ."

"That's eternity for you... the gift that keeps on givin'."

"But we did share some earthly *life* at the same juncture - for a few years at least... ?"

"We did. I'm only sorry that it wasn't spent in the same sphere of influence. We might've been good friends, you and I."

When Derek Hudson appeared, Jefferson's saffron eyes widened with joy. "Hudson my brother, it's been far too long."

"Indeed sir, but it's been difficult finding anyone. You can't imagine the trouble I've had making my way back here... ."

"Certainly I can," Jefferson replied, with a grin. "I've just made a similar journey myself - from my ancestor's home in Abuja, Nigeria to Goiânia, Brazil to here. Took only a few seconds once I knew where I should go."

The two men seemed to blend into and out of one another, as if their specific shapes had no real boundaries any more. I suppose it was only my memory of old black and white images that I'd seen of them that held the men to any specific structure.

"And this fine fellow, who might he be?" Derek wanted to know regarding my being present at their reunion.

"The facilitator I suppose," Jefferson conjectured. "It was his call that you and I chose to answer."

"I'm interested in finding out about your group of artists," I told them. "People I care deeply about are even now investigating Gates' and Faina's little commune of artists."

"A collective is more like it," Sawrey Cockerell corrected, as he suddenly appeared next to me. His past diminutiveness did not truly transcend to this place, for his presence, as I'm sure it was in his life time, was both bold and full-bodied. "We came together in this place to do our work. To build upon each other's egos and fulfill our exhausting need to create."

"Complete our passions is what you mean," Faina Kostadin said, her Macedonian accent still musical. There was an unsymmetrical beauty to her face that no master painter could properly capture. Only a sculptor, working in three-dimensions, could do justice to her unique countenance.

"And to support one another even as the inevitable darkness came nearer and nearer to our life's hearts," Gates Rollins added, taking Faina's hand in hers. Gates, you'll recall, died only two years after they bought this land to live together on. They'd barely completed the house before Faina had to dig her first grave.

"I'm not telling anyone anything new here," Faina replied, recognizing the irony in their shattered desire, "but, you know, the best laid plans and all... ."

"We tried darlin' mine," Gates offered warmly, "I just couldn't keep up my end of the bargain."

Faina, hearing her lover's words, wrapped her sinewy arm around Gates's shoulder and pulled her close - their shimmering shadows suddenly becoming one.

"Our shared room was once a collection of sweet summer songs on soft satin sheets," Gates offered, brimming with nostalgia.

"Or warm winter carols snuggled in deep flannel folds," Faina added, tearfully completing the thought.

"Were you an artist too?" Christabel Gilman asked me the minute she appeared - her form flickering like a faulty incandescent bulb. "I've been listening to you all from afar... ."

"In a different time - yes. I was an artist."

"And were you famous?" she wanted to know next, as all their gazes spun around and landed on me.

"In my fashion," was my answer, "but fame is a relative term. Let's just say that I was able to make a living." There was no need to broadcast my previous celebrity now. That kind of capricious glory deserves no pondering here - death being the great equalizer after all. "People I respected, appreciated my work and that was always enough."

"We all sought fame," Reinhard Ryndes admitted. He was haunting a field of wildflowers just outside the house's old stone foundation. "But it eluded us greatly. Except for maybe Jefferson there. He did rather well in life."

"It's all at the whim of the man," Jefferson knowingly replied. "Very few of my paintin's ever sold durin' my lifetime. And... when they did, the money went directly into the art dealer's pocket."

"None of mine ever sold," Reinhard sadly admitted. "I had to open a business just to have a wall or two to hang my paintings on. Then, I had to start offering food so that people would stay long enough to look at them."

"Van Gogh never sold a painting in his entire lifetime either," I offered, by way of a positive example, and his works sell for millions of dollars today."

"Right," Jefferson agreed, "and he never saw any of that money either."

"And mine?" Reinhard wondered, his face as hopeful as a child's. "Do they claim as high a price as Van Gogh's?"

Gates and Faina smiled in unison at Reinhard's enduring optimism. Even in oblivion's ever darkening tunnel, their friend's fragile ego could only see light.

"Your paintings are about to be hung in a brand new museum," I replied as kindly as I could, "one dedicated solely to your unique collective."

"So, there is a kind of life after death?" Faina offered, with wry smile.

"For all of your existing works - yes."

"Isn't a painting like a novel?" Cicely Norton wondered, glowing with soft intelligence now to my right. "Don't they encapsulate a person, and hold some of their essence even after death?"

"I believe that's true," Jefferson agreed. "Just a phrase or a brushstroke, why even a melody can complete that task."

"Is that why you all painted, or batiked, or sculpted?" I wanted to know. "A chance at immortality?"

"I can't speak for the others," Sawrey answered, "but I created for creation's sake. It was like breathing air or drinking scotch... I couldn't live without it."

"Nor could either of us," Gates added, speaking for Faina as well.

"Reinhard only wanted fame," Derek joked. "It's all he ever talked about. That and selling wine at his new restaurant."

"There was plenty of fine wines to be had there," Reinhard replied, remaining good natured. "You needed a fine wine to put up with having to look at my silly paintings."

"Everything has a price, my dear," Christabel offered, as she floated over to where Reinhard was still haunting. She tried to pick a wildflower as a favor for him, but her fingers just passed right through its stem.

"The price of fame can be far too dear," Sawrey warned, "if you lose your way, you may lose yourself in the bargain."

"There will always be those who do things only for the money," Derek replied knowingly, as false friends had once severely wounded him in their search for riches. "Coming to our little collective saved me... ."

"And me as well," Cicely gratefully admitted.

"The collective was a grand idea," Jefferson added, as he looked fondly at Gates and Faina, who were still swirling and shifting as one. "I only wish that I had some of Reinhard's fine wine right now, so that I could make a proper toast."

"I only wish that I could still taste a fine wine," Sawrey complained lightheartedly. "Being dead has some real downsides."

While I walked among these artists, their combined memories of the time they spent together in this place coalesced, embellishing a bit of that previous void, and suddenly I could almost see their old home - even in its most unsubstantiated form. That ever-shifting spectral vision looked to have had smoked-blue pine shiplap siding, charcoal shutters on each double-hung window, and a steep rouge-grey slate roof. Rhetta's comprehensive investigation certainly implied all these singular facts, so I'm not sure if it was her doing or theirs that put these images into my mind. According to Sawrey and Reinhard's vivid discussion in the spectral parlor, there looked to have been four spacious bedrooms upstairs and two down. As the owners, Gates and Faina were to share one of the first floor rooms and Sawrey the other - mostly so that he wouldn't have to climb the stairs on his short pegs.

At the center of the house was a wide salon, with great high windows. Light was an important thing in the north country, especially when you build your home under a myriad of sprawling pine bows. There was a great mahogany table running down the center of the room - for meals and the laying out of work. In the broad bay window, a set of matching over-stuffed chairs had been set up for private discussions, the playing of chess, or perhaps morning tea.

If there were servants puttering about, Rhetta could find no significant trace of them. It was her conjecture, and I agree, that the collective did for themselves and each other, without any need for such fastidious laborers.

I'm guessing that there was the occasional need for nurses from time to time, as the members of the collective each passed. Oblivion's whisper can be quite frightening for some, and having a kind caregiver there can be quite soothing.

Through Peter's research, he discovered that the reason why all but one of the stones looked alike, was that Reinhard's had come from Ireland. The others with the wee shrugs were all produced locally at the Malone quarry. The last of them being erected by the kind people of Wells, as there was no one left in the collective to bury Cicely Ruth Norton in 1973.

"What did happen to this once spacious house?" I wanted to ask the artists, but then I remembered that none of them were likely alive when the house disappeared. Marvelous Rhetta had a forensic answer to that question as well.

"A propane explosion," she correctly theorized, "took the house somewhere in the early 80's in a deafening BOOM!"

Question: *if a house explodes in the woods and there is no one there to hear it, does it make any noise?*

Rhetta had detected a very faded blast radius, just where the tiny slate chards ended and only pine needles and mushrooms still remained. It was her thought, that after Cicely Norton passed, the house was left forgotten and was clearly abandoned. This wasn't much of a stretch, as anyone that ever loved or cared about the place was now sleeping together beneath the sod. There is no hard evidence, but Rhetta believed that the old piping for the propane tanks slowly corroded over time and began leaking. Where the spark came from is anyone's guess. Maybe it was a lightening bug, I don't know, but an explosion clearly explains where the once stately seven-bedroom house went.

At this time in America, propane was in its so-called golden age, with retail sales reaching well over one billion gallons. With that much volatile gas wafting about, what could go wrong?

There was talk of rebuilding the house as a museum on Saoirse's property overlooking Peter's magnificent view, but there were no photographs or any existing plans to rebuild it from. Again, this is one of the frustrating things about my having become an etherial, even though I know stuff that might be useful, I have absolutely no way of telling my niece what I now know about the house.

Once again, Lorraine came to the rescue - happily offering up our Nutting house as a viable alternative for the museum - which would house the works of the commune's eight singular artists. She felt, and rightly so, that our house was far too big for one old woman to rattle around in and this was a far better use for the place. It would also be a good way to spend-off the obscene amount of money she'd gotten for the Paul Henry painting (the one she'd gotten on the cheap at auction).

"What a fine variety of expression we'll have," she told Saoirse, when Lorraine approached our niece with the idea. "Mr. Hudson produced many fine impressionistic landscapes during his wartime recuperation. They'd be wonderful pieces to hang in our gallery."

"Not to mention any found production sketches of his stage decorations," Saoirse added, catching some of her aunt's burgeoning excitement.

"And Ms. Gilman created some very intriguing photography. I love her work with mothers and daughters. Too bad she never had any children of her own."

"Just as long as you don't pay close attention to the triteness of her critics," Saoirse started to caution, but let the thought go unspoken.

"We've a grand figurative painter in R.C. Ryndes," Lorraine continued, "and it'd be great if we could find some of Sawrey Cockerell's beautiful batiks. There must be some of his fabrics still around."

"Cicely Norton's original illustrations might be hard to locate," Saoirse considered, seeing how all of the woman's art was created for other folk's publications, "but we could certainly use vintage magazine pages as substitute examples... ."

"If need be," Lorraine replied, lost on another thought. "Having her original works would still be best."

"I'm looking forward to seeing some of Faina Kostadin's sculptures. Any idea what they're like? I've not even seen a picture of one."

"*Kostadin's sculptures were known for their compositional dynamism and artistically rounded forms,*" Lorraine recited, having picked up Peter's report on the artist, "*similar to those of her mentor*

Auguste Rodin. After her tenure at the Museum of Fine Arts in Boston, for a short while, Kostadin became an assistant to Rodin himself - creating both hands and legs for some of his sculptures." Then with a gleam in her eye, Lorraine added brightly, "the one piece we should absolutely locate and get for our museum is her masterwork: *"The Muse"*. It was a direct reflection of Rodin's influence, where she used the same model, sitting in the exact same pose as Rodin's *"The Thinker"* - only Faina's figure was a woman."

"Unfortunately, we may have to search all through Macedonia for it," Saoirse added, without sounding the least bit defeated. "I understand that when success failed to find her here in America, Faina sent many of her works back home."

"Then there are Gates Rollins' wonderful pastels," Lorraine noted. "She enjoyed sketching nature scenes, mostly with pools of water in them."

"And our Jefferson Wait," Saoirse continued, "the stalwart fellow that started all this. He also created many impressive Impressionist pieces. We already have yours, and others shouldn't be too hard to locate. He was fairly well respected in his time."

"One of Jefferson's many WPA murals is in a post office in Utica," Lorraine noted. "Maybe we could get Peter to recreate it for us in the hallway there?"

"It's certainly well within his vast capabilities."

Furthering her museum idea, Lorraine asked an old art agent friend of mine to help her identify and locate works that these artists had created, whether they be in private collections or in some donations-oriented thrift store. Thankfully, many of their pieces were found in local homes around Speculator - thus the Museum's name:

The Speculator Foundry Museum of Art.

To make things easier for everyone and hopefully to provide her niece, the sporadic yet gifted writer, with a nice stable income all of her own, Lorraine asked Saoirse if she'd consider managing their new facility.

"You're the one who researched and found all the artists," Lorraine said, trying to convince her. "You're superbly organized and afraid of nothing."

"I believe it was Peter who discovered all the artists, and besides," Saoirse thought it odd that she'd have to remind her, "Chord is still an art teacher at Wainwright Academy down in Redden. Little Rose and I need to be there with him, as his career has value too. Besides, my new book of Cicely Ruth Norton's fairytale illustrations - you know, the missing winter edition that we culled from her magazine work, is taking up all my energies. Between raising Rose Lyric and writing when I can, I don't have much time to myself any more. Why don't you ask Peter to step-up? He'd be grand at it too - at least until some mischievous wind blew him off again into the wild."

"He seems awfully busy with Rhetta these days to be off wandering all on his own," Lorraine replied, not really concerned. "You know that she's taken up full-time residence in my old garage."

"Yeah," Saoirse agreed. "That old parade-float hanger seems like a perfect place for her continued forensic work."

"And profitable too," Lorraine offered. "She wouldn't accept the place as a gift, so her rent money can be put into widening the new museum's parking lot."

"You're always thinkin'."

'They're a good match though, she and him... don'tcha think?"

"They are indeed," Saoirse agreed. "She doesn't let him get away with a damn thing. Just what any overconfident young artist needs on his way to finding true maturity - regular doses of unfettered ego deflation."

"I wish your Uncle Gabe'd had some of that anti-ego medicine," Lorraine cracked wise at my expense - and she was right. I was always so full of myself, at least until Siobhán, Julia, and my dear Lorraine came into my life. There's nothin' like a good woman to polish off a man's rough edges.

If you just let 'em, it's quite enjoyable - trust me.

There was a fine grand opening for the Foundry in April, with many of the eight communal artists' extended families choosing to show up. Some were so taken by Lorraine and Saoirse's handiwork that they decided to become sustaining members right there on the spot - offering their enduring support for such a worthy cause - just so long as their names got put on a plaque or at least something shiny. A few family members actually had art pieces that were created by Lorraine's eight in their homes. That's how she finally snagged an original Sawrey Cockerell batik for the collection. It was resplendent!

Of course the newspaper folks came and went, with most of their self-exalted art critics bent on diminishing these talented folks yet again. "Art is in the eye of the beholder," Lorraine annoyingly responded, after reading a few of their tainted reviews, "and not in some silly pretentious person's unfulfilled expectations of what should have been, instead of what *is*."

There was one or two thoughtful and considerate reviews, where the pundits actually allowed for the work to speak directly from the artist's hand to their unguarded souls - without any preconceived notions or invalid conjectures of what should be. They wanted to be true to the spirit of creation, so they chose to not only allow Sawrey to enthrall them with his magical textile configurations, but to fully embrace both Faina's fluent bronzes, as well as Jefferson's magnificent impressions. They came with their eyes and hearts held open - hoping to be enlightened by what they experienced. Their only expectation was the ability to bathe in someone else's ruminative articulation for a time.

In my mind, it's no different from taking a moment to watch the sun set or follow a shooting star across the night sky. Sure, everyone knows that, like beauty, art is where you find it - but you have to be actively looking for it to even notice it.

Now that all the stories have been told, and you've heard the lot of it, it's time for me to drift away. The best part of being dead is being omnipotent for a while. You get to finally see the big picture. Well, there really isn't a big picture per say, it's just that you get to see everything - the good and the bad all at the same instant. The bad part of that is... you get to see all the good and all the bad in the same instant. Seeing your loved ones in pain and not being able to do anything about it is hell... at least my hell. There's no comforting hand, no warm reassuring embrace, and no words of wisdom.

Nada!

It's not like you can turn away from the horror and survive the moment with a timely blind eye. It's wherever you look. Father Hold-forth at his Sunday pulpit and all his wretched brethren in the choir were wrong about there being a heaven and a hell. There is only acute awareness and a crippling impotency here.

So, earlier I mentioned my grave... it's in Redden, and thanks to the kind generosity of my second wife, I'm happily laying alongside my dear Siobhán in perpetuity. As advertised, Jimmy Ferguson, using a brand new shovel I might add, did a fine job of tucking me into my rectangular sodden-bed for the last time. The stone is the one that I designed for Siobhán, and has a shiny black surface with a tiny bouquet of etched shamrocks near the base. That way, I figured, she'd always have spring flowers.

My concern though is for sweet Lorraine. Where will she go when it's her turn to sleep the big sleep? I used to tease her about having them simply put her in with me. "*What?*" she would reply, feigning shock at even considering such an vile idea, "*and have me sitting on your lap for all eternity?*" What's wrong with that, I would argue, at least you wouldn't be all on your own. Her lighthearted reply to that was always a variation of "s*ure, why not? I'm certain that Siobhán wouldn't mind. That way, we can really get the after-party started.*"

If I ever do locate my Siobhán along this astral plane, I'll have to ask her what she thinks about such a forward-thinking arrangement. My gut suggests that Lorraine is right and she wouldn't mind at all, for Siobhán was always a very thoughtful woman. She'd have wanted me to find love after her passing, and seeing how I was so very fortunate to have found some, Siobhán would've whole-heartedly embraced that bright circumstance. There's no doubt in my mind that she would have liked Lorraine had they ever managed to meet while sharing this mortal coil.

Again, of all the many hurts to being in that grave, was when Peter visited me on the death of his father. Atwell may not've been the greatest of fathers, but his sudden departure left my dear boy an unconsolable orphan - like a small boat listing on the ocean, miles from shore, all alone in the world for the very first time without his choosing. It fractures still my already broken heart to have heard Peter crying out that day, *"Hey! Where are you ol'man?! Where be ya now that I needed ya?!"* Looking back now, I'm not sure which ol'man Peter was shoutin' at - Atwell or me? I'm certain that at some point we both somehow managed to fail him. My shortcomings weren't nearly as intentional as Atwell's, but I suspect they were just slightly less painful for the lad. If Peter'd been a religious fellow, it might also have been a cry out to some supreme being. Though rather young, he'd have guessed that the answer would've been the same one coming from Atwell - nothing.

I was caning my way up the Michigan Avenue steps of The Art Institute of Chicago when I died. There was a lovely retrospective of my work showing in galleries 182 - 184, and as usual, its delinquent creator was late for another opening. Hustling up those stairs at my advanced age proved to be not only my worst idea ever, it heartily implemented my timely demise. A witness later claimed to have seen my actual passing. He reported with some augustness: "*there was this weird glow as if somethin' was on fire, and then, whatever it was suddenly dissipated like a thousand fireflies starting off on a thousand separate journeys. The remaining crumpled shadow was like a mirror in the darkness. It was without any shape at all - being mostly the absence of Chicago.*" I'm not certain if the onlooker was drunk, high, or simply an illustrative overachiever, but I'm glad someone besides those damn laughing bronze lions saw me off to oblivion.

Entering the Redden cemetery, visitors pass by a rather theatrical white marble tableau of Jesus surrounded by a few of his earthbound angels. It's quite dramatic - or traumatic, depending on your informed or not so informed perspective. For me, being raised Catholic, it is simply Christ hanging on the cross. Something that I'd seen in every room of my childhood friend Wilmer Morrison's house. Something his mother and his aunts spoke so freely to, but never heard any answer from. It was part of the silver necklaces and religious brooches that the girls I most admired in high school wore - only my thoughts regarding their necklines were more carnal in nature. For others, say an alien being from Alpha Centauri or even some newly discovered local aborigine culture stepping up to such a display, it might be absolutely horrifying. Imagine, being a sentient being and seeing that harsh representation of a man having been nailed to a wooden post by his hands for the first time. Even with minimal contemplation, that image would be quite telling, especially in regards to mankind's profound level of cruelty for a fellow human. That poor skewered fellow didn't get into that predicament all on his own. He'd need three hands for that. So... any alien would be correct in assuming that we Earth folks were not only rather mean spirited in nature, but that they should be quite wary of our level of expressed hate. I know Jesus represents love for most of his followers, but there's little evidence of that grand compassion when one first looks at that stark marble tableau. That dichotomy still strikes me each time I enter the cemetery. Being on this side, and never having seen Jesus, doesn't surprise me. I suspect Wilmer's mother and her sister felt the exact same way when they all arrived here.

My other thoughts, when my mind can focus, go out to Eugene and Sile. May they find life as not so difficult a journey as it might be. No life is ever free of shite, 'cause bad things are bound to happen - even to the best of folks. Chaos's provocative randomness will surly provide plenty of such opportunities for both pain as well as reciprocal joy. But, they're a grand couple, who seem to see their road ahead as a lively two-step dance. Always being able to hear the same musical accompaniment, makes the grand masquerade all that much easier.

As for me grandsons Andrew and Aaron, *may the road rise up to meet them, with warm sunshine forever on their sweet faces, and a gentle wind of confidence always pushing at their backs.* I'm sad at not being there to influence them myself, but Eugene quotes me well and often enough so that I'm there in word if not in deed.

Maybe, one day, if I'm dead long enough, perhaps more of these standoffish etherials will choose to talk to me. It's not like we're a big coalition of ghosts or anything. Right now, they are simply vivid memories of my loved ones, passed friends, and a billion strangers.

As you may have noticed, finding anyone around here is the real nightmare. It's not like St. Peter is sitting in a beach chair at the Golden Gates handing out seating charts. This alternate plane of consciousness is freakin' massive. Consider all the folks that have died since the beginning of time - including for example: the Taiping Rebellion (100 million), World War I (65 million), and World War II (72 million), the Russian Civil War (9 million) and the damn Napoleonic Wars (7 million) and that's who's wandering free around this place. To make matters worse, an awful lot of 'em look alike, what with all their splendid brass buttons, service medals, and military epaulettes and all. Wait... it just occurred to me... there's not one single Nazi here. Not one. I wonder where all those assholes got off to?

So, for all practical purposes, there's mostly just spirits everywhere - well forces of nature really, not so much in any physical form as I may have led you to believe. Breezes with faces they are, and I'll find me my boy Micheal and my darlin' Siobhán if it takes forever.

There's things they need to hear.

Often, after relating such profundity, my brain drifts away from all conscious thought, and an old nursery rhyme fills that space in my head. The verses swirl round and around - finally fading away:

I am a torn sail,

a forgotten tale,

yesterday's mail,

a lost holy grail,

a windless gale,

an empty pail,

a flooded dale,

a keyless jail

a ripped vail,

a vacant rail,

a bent nail,